T0064299

When Love Knocks

Carolyn J. Pollack

Order this book online at www.trafford.com
or email orders@trafford.com

Most Trafford titles are also available at major online book retailers.

Printed in the United States of America.

ISBN: 978-1-4907-3554-2 (sc)
ISBN: 978-1-4907-3556-6 (hc)
ISBN: 978-1-4907-3555-9 (e)

Library of Congress Control Number: 2014908471

Trafford rev. 05/07/2014

www.trafford.com

North America & international
toll-free: 1 888 232 4444 (USA & Canada)
fax: 812 355 4082

Acknowledgements

Ms Marie Seeman has graciously allowed me to mention her name and allude to one of her paintings "Country Road" in "When Love Knocks". If you would like to view more of Marie's art you are encouraged to go to her website:

www.marieseemanart.com

Also, mentioned in "When Love Knocks" is a company called **Music Box Attic.** This company manufactures exquisite musical boxes. I ordered one in 2013. As soon as I saw my music box I immediately knew I wanted Adam to give one to Dylan. I contacted Boris from Music Box Attic asking permission to do this and was told yes.

They can be reached at:

Music Box Attic, www.musicboxattic.com
7346 Radford Ave,
North Hollywood,
California,
USA 91605

Chapter One

Dylan jumped easily from the saddle while her horse side-stepped gingerly, not liking the abrupt halt she'd been forced to make. "Steady girl, this won't take a minute." Dylan patted her mare's glossy neck, trying to quieten the prancing animal. She tried to look into the bushes where the stealthy movements had caught her eye in the first place. There was an overpowering stench that threatened to drive her away, but Dylan was adamant; this time, she was going to search the area. She was certain she'd found the object of her search. She tried holding her breath to hold the horrible smell at bay, but was soon forced to exhale, much to her disgust.

"Just as I thought," she smiled exaltedly as she spied the small grey furry animal that was trying unsuccessfully to hobble away from her. It was a baby kangaroo. It couldn't be more than a few months old; it should still be in its mother's pouch.

"Come on, little one, I don't know about you, but I'd like to get out of here." The joey's mother was dead. Her rotting carcass was fouling the air with its stench. The surrounding air was alive with buzzing blowflies and Dylan thought she'd be sick if she didn't get away soon. She bundled the tiny marsupial into the hessian bag she'd been carrying with her on her rides lately. She was elated that she'd found the tiny orphan alive, her hopes had been fading. She quickly hefted herself back up into the saddle, "Come on, Sascha, let's get out of here."

Tom will have to come back and bury the mother, Dylan thought, as she made her way back to the farmyard, but at least this little one is safe. She'd seen the joey on the last few occasions that she'd been out riding, but until now he'd proved to be an elusive shadow when it came to being caught. *He must be weak and hungry for me to have gotten this close to him,* Dylan thought. She couldn't believe her luck.

Dylan was met by her friend, Rae, when she rode into the farm yard. "Rae, I found him. The poor little thing is starving," she exclaimed excitedly, handing the bag carefully to her friend as she dismounted.

Rae opened the bag to look inside, finding exactly what she'd expected . . . a baby kangaroo.

"If it was left up to you, we'd have every stray animal and bird in the neighbourhood housed in our barn. What am I supposed to do with him?"

"Feed him like you do with all of the rest. You know as well as I do that you've got a soft spot for everything on this place . . . starting with him," Dylan jerked her thumb towards the man who was walking towards them.

"Did someone call me?" joked Tom coming to see what was going on.

"Hello, my Darling," Rae said adoringly to her husband. She opened the bag showing him what it contained, "meet our new boarder."

"Great," Tom declared, with as much enthusiasm as he would have shown for crutching sheep, "I'll go and show the kids; at least they'll find it fascinating."

"Wonderful man, your husband," Dylan stated drolly, indicating his retreating figure as he walked back to the barn.

"I think so."

The two friends smiled at each other fondly. "Come on, help me with Sascha. I'm dying for a cup of tea," Dylan said, already undoing the girth on the saddle. She added light-heartedly, "I'll bring you up to date on the 'let's find Dylan a lover' plan the girls at work have got going. Honestly, you'd think they'd give it a rest, wouldn't you?"

"Why?" Rae replied, grinning at the outraged expression her answer had produced on her friend's face.

"You know why!" Dylan flatly refused to budge from the stand she'd taken on this particular subject. It was about the only thing that she and Rae ever argued about. She was beginning to regret bringing the subject up now.

"Come on, Dylan, if we're going to have one of our discussions, let it be on a full stomach," Rae marched around the mare's rump, linking her arm through Dylan's and proceeded to pull her towards the house, "I made some scones while you were out riding."

"Rae, you're . . ." Dylan stated, but the rest of her sentence wasn't uttered as Rae interjected.

"Yes, I know, I'm impossible." Rae had heard it all before.

As a divorced woman Dylan was considered fair game. Rae could understand why she'd be cautious, even picky, but to turn down every single offer she'd had in the two years since her divorce, that she couldn't fathom. Dylan had hidden her emotions very carefully, not letting any man come close to her. Certainly not close enough to see the warm, vibrant person beneath that artificial, cold veneer she'd woven around herself. Rae despaired of ever seeing her friend truly happy again. They were sitting on the verandah at the back of Rae's house; this was where most of their discussions seemed to take place. It was peaceful sitting here, seeing the mountain ranges in the background. They were so near, and yet so far away. Everything between those ranges and the house belonged to Rae and Tom. The paddocks dotted with the black and white cattle which made up their dairy herd, were lush and green. The horses, hers amongst them, were few at the present time, but if things worked out as Tom hoped, he'd branch out into breeding a few horses in a few more years. There was a creek, Dylan couldn't see it from where she sat, but its course was marked by the gum trees growing along its banks. They were nourished by the cool, clear water and stood straight and tall.

Dylan loved it here. The tranquility sheltered her when she was hurting and when there was happiness to share, there was Rae.

At the moment, Rae was being anything but friendly as she told her friend, "Because of your old fashioned ideas, every man will pass you by."

Dylan shook her head vehemently, "I don't care. I don't want casual sex. Just because I won't jump into bed with every man I meet, I'm being condemned for it. Anyway, I don't see anyone throwing themselves off a cliff over me, either," she finished defensively. She certainly wasn't against sex, but she wasn't going to degrade herself by having shallow affairs or one night stands under the very noses of her children either, and that's what would happen. Most men didn't want the responsibility of another man's family. This was the first lesson she'd learnt after her divorce. She'd rather be alone, living with the frustration of an empty bed every night. She felt she owed it to her children and to herself to stick to her principles. *What was sex anyway!*

"Maybe so," Rae reflected. She understood why Dylan was taking this line of reasoning, but darn it all, she was too young and beautiful to lock herself away. She continued, "Surely there's been someone you've been attracted to since your divorce?"

"Nope," Dylan answered slowly, "It looks like I'll become an old maid. I'll invest in some cats and come and live with you and Tom. Isn't that what old maids do?" Her blue eyes twinkled mischievously, as she glanced at Rae.

"Over my dead body, to both of your suggestions," Rae threw back at her, "and here come three perfectly good reasons why not, right now."

Dylan looked in the direction of Rae's stare and found herself looking into the faces of her three children as they made their way towards the verandah where the two women sat. Reaching out to take Dylan's hand in hers, Rae gently asked, "Are you sure it's not fear that's stopping you from making another commitment to a man?" She gave Dylan's hand a reassuring squeeze, before letting it go.

Dylan was saved from answering by the arrival of her children. They were all clamouring for food and drink, but as usual Rae had given her something to think about. The trouble with Rae was she judged every man by Tom's standards. He was a wonderful husband and probably her best friend to boot. Dylan was constantly telling her that the mould had been broken after Rae had married Tom.

Rae and Tom's dairy was situated fifteen kilometres north of the township of Deception Bay, where Dylan lived with her three young children. Their farm was virtually secluded from the rest of society and they'd always maintained that they were very happy with their seclusion. On one boundary, far to the west they were flanked by low mountain ranges while their other boundaries formed the beginnings of a massive state pine forest which, according to Rae, went on forever making the perfect foil between them and the rest of civilisation. The main state highway was only minutes away, but because of the pine forest it was permanently hidden from view. Dylan found her friends' farm to be the perfect retreat when she needed to get away from the worries the rest of the world threw at her from time to time. Rae and Tom had the added advantage of being close to the rapidly growing cities of Redcliffe to the south and Caboolture to the north, both of which were only about a twenty minute drive in either direction on the Bruce highway. If ever they needed to go into Brisbane, it was only an hour's leisurely drive down the highway to the south. Thinking about it, Dylan thought the same could be said about herself and the little township of Deception Bay where she lived.

Deception Bay had the distinct privilege, in Dylan's opinion, of being in the heart of a thriving farming community, though of late there had been a massive building boom in the area that was threatening to overtake the dozens of hobby farmers who had settled here many years ago. Some of the state forest had been cut down to make way for new housing estates, which were starting to spring up all over the place. It was the perfect location having the ocean on one side and the farming community on the other.

Dylan thought she had the best of both worlds there for the taking right on her doorstep. She and her children made frequent trips to the beach, but Dylan had to secretly admit to herself that her heart would always be firmly entrenched in the land.

They had arranged to have a bar-b-que tea. It had become a pleasant ritual to go over to Rae's place most Sundays. Dylan's horses were agisted here which made it possible for her to go riding whenever she pleased. Rae was also her baby-sitter when Dylan went to work during the week. This arrangement suited them both. Rae loved Dylan's children almost as much as Dylan did herself. In fact, Rae and Tom were godparents to all three of Dylan's children.

Shortly after they'd finished tea, Dylan helped clean up and then said tiredly, "I think I might make tracks for home. It's been a long day and I'm tired. Besides it's time you two had some time to yourselves."

"Don't preach what you don't practice," Rae threw back at her. She was sitting on Tom's lap with her head leaning comfortably against his shoulder. They looked the perfect couple and indeed they were. Dylan loved them both.

"I'll think about it," she lied, thinking, *anything for a bit of peace.*

The following week was a busy one. Dylan worked as a Librarian. One of the libraries in town was short staffed and as Dylan was the person who was usually picked to fill in the gaps during these times, she found herself juggling her time between both places of work. This meant less time with her family and so on an impulse she made a stop at a family restaurant, using their drive-thru facility to select the food they would eat. It was Friday and Dylan was contemplating a quiet relaxing time at home with her young family.

There was a cartoon movie on television tonight and Dylan had been persuaded into letting her trio stay up to watch it. She wouldn't exactly call it quality time spent with her family, but she would make up for it over the week-end. They were going to visit Dylan's parents' this weekend which usually meant a trip to the beach. Bribie Island was just a short drive away in the car. This was always an enjoyable visit and it also gave Dylan a chance to see her parents.

"Come on, you two, it's time for bed," Dylan said, looking affectionately at her two sons. Two pairs of eyes looked up at her; one child had blue eyes like hers, while the other had brown eyes which was a legacy from his father.

"Do we have to yet, Mummy?" Danny asked, while trying to stifle the yawn that threatened to undermine his request.

"Yes, you do. Now scram," Dylan answered with tolerant amusement as she followed them down the hallway to the room they shared. She listened to all of their last minute requests as she tucked them into bed. They'd made her promise that the proposed trip to Nan's wouldn't be called off even if it did rain as it was threatening to do. Already, there was the occasional flash of lightning followed by a loud boom of thunder. *At least if it did rain, it would cool things down a bit,* Dylan thought. She felt the perspiration trickle down her back, reminding her of how hot it was at present.

Dylan went to check on the youngest of her children, her daughter, Natalie. She was two years old. Dylan watched the gentle rise and fall of her chest as she slept. She thought once again how like Jake she was in looks. She had the same dark brown hair and brown eyes as her ex-husband. *I only hope she doesn't grow up to have his rotten nature,* Dylan thought bitterly, thinking of the man who had walked out on her after their daughter had been born. How could anyone look at this beautiful child and say she wasn't his daughter? Dylan had been heartbroken at the time. She'd loved Jake and the life they'd shared together. *Anyway,* she determined, *that was a long time ago. I've made another life for myself now, one that's free and clear of the complications that being in love can bring.*

"Yes, but that doesn't make up for the times when you wake up in an empty bed, yearning for the tender touch of a man, or for the times when you yearn for someone to hold you, ending in fulfilling lovemaking," Dylan told herself sadly. It had been so long. *Maybe when the children are older I'll think about it,* she thought sighing sadly.

"Come on, girl," Dylan admonished herself severely. "It's not that bad, is it? A lot of people would love to have what you have; three beautiful children, plus a roof over your head; one that you'll own one day. You have a job you love, one that gives you plenty of time to spend with your family." The bills were pretty much under control too, if she thought about it. Life was pretty good at the moment.

Glancing at the paper after she'd returned to the lounge room, Dylan saw she had just enough time to have a shower and make herself a cup of coffee, before the late movie was due to begin. "And so ends another perfect week," she muttered half-heartedly to herself as she walked towards the bathroom.

Undressing, Dylan looked at herself in the mirror. Addressing herself critically, she remarked, "I'm not in bad shape for someone who's had three children." Her reflection showed a mature woman of twenty-seven with firm, full breasts and a trim waist. She was tall, with long legs that showed a healthy tan from long hours spent in the sun. Looking at her face, she saw twinkling blue eyes, a straight nose and a mobile mouth that was always ready to smile. Her face was framed by light brown curls, worn short in an attempt to master them, but more often than not, this attempt failed miserably.

Settling down later with a cup of coffee, Dylan realised she'd seen this particular movie before. She wasn't all that keen to sit through it again, because as she remembered, it had a lousy ending which she thought spoilt the entire show. Turning the television off, Dylan's attention was caught by car headlights as they swung in a wide arc in front of her house. She didn't take any notice, thinking it was probably someone driving into her neighbour's yard across the road. That was what Dylan liked about living here, because although she had neighbours across the way, there weren't any houses on her side of the street. This afforded her complete privacy.

Hearing a knock at her door, Dylan realised the car headlights meant the visitors were for her. Wondering who could be calling at this hour, she opened the door, expecting to see one of her friends standing there, or perhaps a member of her family who needed a bed for the night. Instead, there was a perfect stranger standing on her doorstep making Dylan acutely conscious of the fact that she was only clothed in a flimsy nightgown which, by her own admission, had seen better days, but it was comfortable and Dylan liked it, although she conceded, it offered little protection from prying eyes should anyone feel the need to look more closely. She bereted herself silently for not having chosen more appropriate sleepwear, but how was she to know she'd receive visitors at this late hour. She quickly covered herself with the lace curtain that hung across the sliding glass doors.

"Yes, can I help you?" Dylan asked the man standing there. She tried to put a note of authority into her voice, to cover the fact that she was nervous; after all, it wasn't every night she had a handsome man knock on her door. And handsome he was! Dylan surprised herself with the amount of detail her brain gathered in that one swift glance. He had light brown hair, similar in colour to her own. It was collar length and stylishly cut. His green eyes were looking at her with a touch of amusement. No doubt because of the curtain she was now trying to cover herself with. He was having trouble trying not to smile, Dylan noted to herself wryly, but in the end, good manners won out and he was able to school his features into a more serious mode.

"I was hoping I might be able to use your phone? I'm afraid I can't get any reception on my cell phone." He held his phone up in the palm of his hand, before continuing, "I'm having car trouble. It's a hire car so I don't have any tools with me. I have people expecting me to-night. I'd like to let them know I haven't gotten myself lost. Yours is the only house in the street I could see with some lights on."

He had a deep baritone voice and spoke with an American accent, although just what part of the States he was from Dylan couldn't guess. She looked at him, wondering if she should let him come into her home. The isolation that she'd been praising just a short time ago could work against her, if her instincts were wrong and this man proved to be dangerous.

These thoughts must have showed on Dylan's face, because he stated calmly, "You can trust me Mrs . . ." putting emphasis on the Mrs so that Dylan felt compelled to supply her last name.

"It's Miles. Dylan Miles," Dylan answered.

"Well, Mrs Miles, you can trust me. Now, could I use that phone?" he asked again.

"Alright," Dylan answered, still feeling a bit apprehensive, "come in. The phone's over there on the wall." She indicated to the lounge room wall with a flick of her hand then added quickly as a thought struck her, "If you'll excuse me, I'll just go and put on something more appropriate." Now why on earth had she told him that? All she'd done was draw attention to the fact that she was scantily dressed, but the smile he was trying so hard to hide bore testimony to the fact that he'd already noticed that one small fact anyway.

He followed her inside, and then walked towards the phone, saying as he did so, "Don't change on my account. You look fine." He smiled broadly as he spoke, treating Dylan to a grin that had her scuttling down the hallway to her bedroom where she quickly donned her ancient dressing gown. *What have I done,* she thought wildly? He could be a maniac and she'd let him in. It was a few minutes before she had the courage to go back out to face him. After all, she reasoned, it would be better to face him in the lounge room rather than the bedroom. Her glance strayed to the bed, while her mind flashed with vivid pictures of them in the act of making love. Her body went hot with the thought of it. She tried to stop her body's reaction to this ridiculous situation in which she found herself. *You ridiculous fool,* she told herself sternly, *of all the stupid things to think about. Only you could find yourself attracted to an absolute stranger, one who could be waiting, even now, to mug you as you walk back out, and what about the children . . .*

Dylan was relieved to find him still on the phone when she returned to the lounge room. He was leaning casually against the wall with his back to her, obviously listening to the person on the other end of the line. She found she was able to look at him, without his being aware of her interest. He was tall and Dylan guessed his height to be about six foot three inches. He had broad shoulders that tapered down to slim hips and very long legs that were covered with firm fitting blue denim jeans. She could see the muscles ripple under his shirt as he moved slightly, shifting his weight from one leg to the other. He turned suddenly to face her. Dylan was embarrassed to be caught in the act of ogling him. She could feel herself colouring under his steady scrutiny of her.

He looks tired, Dylan thought, as she watched him drag a hand through his hair. He covered the mouthpiece of the phone with one of his hands, before asking her, "Would you mind if I gave my friends your address and phone number? They'll need to know where to pick me up."

Dylan heard herself supplying the information he required, so that he could pass it on to the voice on the other end of the line.

Shortly afterwards, he hung up the receiver. Dylan watched him walk over to where she was sitting. He towered over her. She felt suddenly shy, as she gazed up into his handsome face. She felt lost for words, so she waited for him to start some kind of intelligent conversation. It struck her then that he looked strangely familiar, which was ridiculous. She racked her brains trying to think where she knew him from before finally telling herself that if she knew him, his would be a face that she'd never forget in a hurry.

"Well, I guess you heard most of that, Mrs Miles?" he stated matter-of-factly, as he looked down at her.

"Yes. Will it be a while before your friends can pick you up?" Dylan couldn't quite stop the wobble that affected her voice. She hoped he hadn't been able to detect its presence.

"It looks that way, possibly not before morning. It seems they've been drinking. I'll sleep in the car. It won't be the first time I've had to rough it. It's only for a few hours anyway," he said looking down at her, noticing the way her hair curled around her head in an unruly mass. He thought it looked very becoming.

Running a hand through his own hair, he started to thank her for the use of the phone. Outside, a bright flash of lightning could be seen illuminating the dark sky. It was followed shortly afterwards by loud rumbling thunder. The rain started to fall then, slowly at first, but getting louder in volume until Dylan thought she'd go deaf.

"Well, you can't go out in this downpour. Would you like a cup of coffee while you wait for the storm to pass?" Dylan inquired, indicating with her hands, towards the sky. She realised she was holding her breath as she waited for his answer. Standing up, she noticed she only came to his shoulder. This fact pleased her somehow, being somewhat tall herself, five feet eight inches. Dylan mentally chided herself for having such a silly thought. After tonight, she'd never see him again. This saddened her, for already she felt drawn to this man.

"If you're sure it's no bother, yes, I wouldn't mind a cup of coffee. I guess I should introduce myself seeing we're going to share coffee." His voice sounded like a caress, sending a pleasurable tingle down Dylan's spine. He treated her to a dazzling smile that had her insides quivering with excitement.

"I'm Adam Rossiter." He held out his hand, so Dylan felt compelled to put her own hand into his. She felt again those delicious tingles up and down her spine. Her heart had started to beat faster, *most probably due to nerves,* Dylan thought, trying to find a logical excuse for the feelings she was experiencing. She quickly withdrew her hand from his, nervously wiping it down the side of her dressing gown. After all, it wasn't every night she had a stranger knock on her door; one who was then invited into her home and then asked to stay for coffee.

Asking him to sit down, Dylan walked into the kitchen and began her task. She couldn't help thinking about the phone conversation he'd had earlier. She wondered about the people he'd spoken to, whether they were Australian like herself or American like he was. She couldn't think of anything to say to him as she busied herself in the kitchen, so she remained silent. She wondered if any of her neighbours had seen him arrive. One neighbour in particular, Jo, Dylan swore had eyes in the back of her head. She'd probably make it her business to find out who Dylan's late night visitor was.

Smiling to herself, Dylan could see her friend in her mind's eye, quizzing her relentlessly about her visitor. If only she had the answers to the questions her friend would ask, not for Jo's sake, but for her own curiosity. She'd like to know more about this man, who after only a very short acquaintance could make Dylan respond to him, without his even being aware of it.

She jumped with fright when a deep masculine voice intruded into her thoughts to ask casually, "What's so funny?" She turned to see him watching her from the doorway.

Feeling acutely embarrassed, Dylan explained about her nosy neighbour, and then added hastily, "Jo's okay, but she can be a bit intrusive at times. I guess it goes with her outgoing personality."

"Are you saying that you haven't got an outgoing personality, Dylan?" he wanted to know, emphasising her name as he said it for the first time.

"No, not exactly," answered Dylan shyly. She looked up at him and then quickly averted her gaze. She liked the way her name had sounded on his lips thinking his accent gave it a special caress. *This man is weaving a spell over me,* she thought. I can't seem to keep my mind or my eyes off him. She proved her point by spilling hot coffee over her fingers, as she handed him the scalding drink.

Taking the cup from her trembling fingers, he proceeded to run her hand under the cold water tap, massaging her fingers as he did so. It was all Dylan could do to keep her hand in his grasp. She found it took all of her willpower to act naturally and let him minister to the burn which could be seen forming on her fingers.

After a moment or so, he pronounced glibly, "I don't think there's any permanent damage. I'm sure you'll be able to use it again sometime soon." Having said this, he reached for a tea towel and proceeded to carefully wipe the water from her hand with a sensual slowness that had Dylan's mind reeling from the unexpected gentleness of his touch.

"Thank you, it's fine now. I'm sure I'll live," she lied, needing to put some space between them. She'd rather endure the pain from the burn, than suffer the sweet torture that his touch was inflicting onto her raw nerve endings.

Adam broke the silence that was threatening to engulf them, by asking suddenly, "Shouldn't you be more concerned about what your husband will say when he arrives home to find me here, or at least out in the car, before you worry yourself about some gossiping neighbour." He was looking intently at her, almost as if her answer was important to him.

"I'm divorced," Dylan stated reluctantly. She immediately thought that perhaps she should have kept this particular piece of information to herself for fear he might turn out to be dangerous. Maybe she should have invented a husband because if he thought she had a husband who was due home, he'd drink his coffee and go out to his car to wait for his friends. Dylan realised with some surprise that within her heart, she'd wanted him to know about her marital status.

Some of the apprehension Dylan was feeling must have shown on her face, because he gave a slight chuckle saying, "Dylan, don't be afraid of me. I'm not the sort of man to take advantage of a situation like this. I appreciate your hospitality very much. Opening your door to a complete stranger these days can be dangerous. Besides, I'm too tired to even think of anything like that."

When he saw the look of uncertainty that Dylan gave him, he sent her a quick smile, adding, "That was supposed to be a joke. Come on, let's sit down and have our coffee."

"Oh, yes, sorry, please sit down," Dylan gestured, leading the way to the kitchen table. Once seated, she was at a loss for words and momentarily sat gazing into her cup. When the silence threatened to stretch ahead of them forever, she asked the first thing that came into her head, wanting to know why he was in Australia.

"I'm working over here for a few months, with a bit of sight-seeing thrown in when time permits," he replied casually, looking at Dylan to see what her reaction was to such a non-committal answer.

"In other words, it's none of my business and you don't want to talk about it," her curiosity was well and truly roused now as she waited for his answer.

"Something like that. How about you, what do you do when you're not helping out stranded strangers?" He deliberately turned the conversation around, so she was forced to tell him about herself.

"Well," answered Dylan, putting her head to one side as she spoke. She was thinking of the hectic days she spent working and trying to bring up her family as a single mum, "I do a little bit of everything, I guess."

Before she could go on, he looked at her and asked, "Everything. Just what does everything mean?"

Gazing at him across the table, Dylan could see he was smiling at her again. *It's a good thing I won't be seeing him again after this. I could start to like having this man around the place,* Dylan thought a little sadly. He seems to be the sort of man who could get anything he wanted from a woman without any real effort at all.

"Dylan?" he prompted, with a questioning glance.

"Nothing very spectacular, I'm afraid. I'm a librarian. I work at the local library. I like to ride horses; I own a couple. Friends of mine look after them for me. Also, I have three children," Dylan looked at Adam's face, trying to fathom what his reaction would be to this last piece of information.

"Three," he responded, holding up three fingers as he whispered the word. He'd been going to ask about her work as a librarian, but upon hearing that this beautiful woman sitting opposite him was the mother of three children; the other questions were chased from his mind.

"Three," confirmed Dylan. She didn't know it, but her face softened as she thought of her children who were sleeping peacefully in their respective beds.

She hoped he wouldn't make reference to the rather worn out comment most men threw at her when they were informed she was the mother of three children. It rankled her beyond belief. "Surely not!" they would say which was usually followed by, "But you don't look old enough to have three children."

"Tell me about them. Are they as pretty as their mother?" he inquired softly.

Like any parent Dylan didn't need any urging when it came to talking about her offspring. Suppressing the thrill of happiness his backhanded compliment had given her, she launched into a narrative about her children.

"Danny is five. He started Prep this year. At the moment, all he ever talks about is having a motorbike. He feels he's old enough to handle one on his own." Dylan lapsed into silence as her mind recalled the defiant stance Danny had put up when she'd told him he'd have to wait a few more years before that particular dream became a reality. She was secretly hoping by then that he'd have changed his mind about the bike, but if not, well, he'd at least be older and stronger and hopefully, more capable of handling a bike like the one he wanted.

"Tell me about the other two?" Adam urged her to continue.

"Aren't you bored yet? Most men would be by now."

"No," he whispered softly, willing Dylan to go on.

"Glen is four. He looks like his father," Dylan was unaware of the change in her voice as she mentioned her ex-husband. Adam glanced at her, seeing the hardness that had come into her eyes. He said nothing. "He's a real pet. Natalie has just turned two. She's at the difficult stage, the terrible two's and into everything," Dylan finished lamely, wishing she could still talk. At least then, she wasn't so nervous.

"It sounds like you have your hands full," he commented, as he stood up to take their empty cups into the kitchen.

Dylan followed him, watching absently as he rinsed the cups under the tap. His hands looked so capable, so big. Dylan found herself wondering what it would be like to be touched by those hands. *Whoa! Stop!* She put her riotous thoughts on hold, not believing the dangerous road they'd been leading her down. *Heavens, we're perfect strangers,* she thought to herself. *It must have something to do with the fact that I've been alone for so long . . .*

"Well, that's all done, so I guess I'd better be going."

Adam's words interrupted her volatile thoughts. He was giving her a strange look. Had her thoughts been so obvious to him? Was she that transparent? Dylan couldn't remember clearly afterwards who made the first move. All she knew was the next moment she was in Adam's arms and he was kissing her. What was more, she was kissing him back. A deep passionate kiss that stirred up emotions Dylan thought she'd buried forever. His tongue probed the soft contours of her mouth, seeming to do an inventory of the delights he found there. This handsome stranger had opened the floodgates of Dylan's heart. Floodgates she'd thought she'd safely dammed forever.

When they finally released each other, Dylan couldn't look at him. She could feel a tell-tale blush creeping up her neck and onto her face.

"I'm sorry, Dylan. I don't know what came over me," Adam confessed shaking his head ever so slightly as he looked down at her. "Am I forgiven?" he queried, as he lifted her chin up gently with his little finger. He wanted to see her face when she answered.

Dylan found her throat was constricted with pent up emotion. She was only able to nod her head thereby letting him know his kiss had been welcomed. Her passion for this man frightened her; if he was to suggest making love, she knew she'd gladly agree. This shocked her, because she was basically a person of principle, never taking risks on anything, let alone a man she'd just met . . . how long ago . . . maybe an hour. Could a person fall in love that quickly?

Unaware of Dylan's thoughts Adam said, "It's funny how you just seem to click with someone, isn't it? I feel comfortable in your company, Dylan."

"Just like a pair of old slippers, that's me," Dylan ventured and they both laughed.

"You know when you first came to the door tonight, I felt as if I knew you, but I know we've never met before." She was surprised to see a look of concern pass fleetingly over his handsome features, but it disappeared so swiftly, she thought she must have imagined it.

"Kismet. I think I would have remembered you if we'd ever met before," Adam told her softly. His green eyes roamed over her face, stopping to rest on the soft lips that his lips had only moments before caressed.

"It's still pouring outside," Dylan stated, turning the conversation around to something she considered to be a much safer topic, "If you want, you can spend the night in the spare room. At the moment, it's used as a play room, but there's a bed in there you could use." Holding her breath, she waited for his answer, expecting a polite, but very firm, no, followed by a quick exit out of the door. *This is stupid,* she thought; *I don't want him to leave . . . ever.*

Adam stood looking down at her. Dylan assumed he was trying to think of a way out. She couldn't judge from his expression what his thoughts were. Another clap of thunder boomed overhead as Adam spoke, nearly drowning out his softly spoken words, "Thank you, I think I'll accept your kind offer."

Dylan was about to show him where he was to sleep, when one of his hands snaked out, stopping her in mid stride. "Just one more thing," A slow smile started to spread across his handsome features as he watched Dylan's face for her reaction to his next words, "Will I be perfectly safe? I mean, I don't know you very well, do I."

Dylan stared up at him as the implication of his words slowly sunk into her befuddled brain. He was obviously making a reference to the kiss they'd shared, but she was sure that he was also letting her know that she could trust him not to take advantage of the situation his staying would place her in. She could feel the crimson blush spreading over her face as she searched her mind for an appropriate answer, "You'll be perfectly safe. I haven't walked in my sleep in years," she told him at last.

"Pity," Adam told her dryly.

Dylan felt strangely happy as she led Adam down the hallway to the room where he would sleep. She preceded him into the room saying, "It's going to be Nat's room when I fix it up."

"Where does she sleep now, in with the boys?"

"She's still in a cot in my room," Dylan replied, as she stooped to pick up some toys from the floor. She looked quickly away from the bed, as her mind pictured him there.

"It'll be fine," Adam looked intently at Dylan as she stood before him. She was clutching a battered, yellow teddy bear in her arms. She had to look hastily away for fear of betraying her turbulent emotions. *I must be mad, but I almost wish something would happen so we could make love,* she thought to herself.

"Well, I'll leave you to it. I'll get you a towel if you want to take a shower. The bathroom's over there. The boys wake up early. I hope you don't like to sleep in. Maybe you should've knocked on someone else's door, after all."

"I'm glad I knocked on your door, Dylan. Are all Australians as hospitable as you are?" Adam asked her with a gleam in his eyes, no doubt thinking back to the kiss they'd shared earlier.

"I've no idea," was all Dylan could think of to say in answer to his obvious taunt, as yet another blush covered her tanned face with a crimson hue. The last thing she wanted was for him to think he was on to a good thing, but given her behaviour of the last hour what else could he possibly think.

"I've never known anyone to blush as much as you do. Does this happen with every person you talk to, or have I cornered the market?" laughed Adam, reaching out to casually run his fingers down Dylan's cheek.

"It's very unusual. Most people would've said nothing and not embarrassed me," Dylan answered, trying to make a joke of the situation.

"You look very becoming when you blush and I'm not most people." He started towards her, but suddenly stopped himself, telling her as he did so that he thought it would be better if she was to leave before he completely lost what little control he had left over his seething emotions.

Dylan opened her mouth to contradict him, only stopping herself at the last minute, knowing he was right. "Good night, then. I'll see you in the morning," having said this, she turned and left the room, knowing that if she stayed, she'd be lost.

Adam watched her leave, his hands clenched tightly at his sides. When he finally made his way to the bathroom, he made sure he had the house to himself. He'd seen the light go out from under Dylan's door, just seconds before. A shower was just what he needed, but he muttered quietly to himself as he turned on the tap, "I think I'd better make it a cold one."

Chapter Two

"Mummy! Mummy! There's a person in the bedroom," shouted an excited little voice in Dylan's ear.

"Mummy, wake up. Do you think it's a burglar? Should we call the police?"

"No, Glen, I know who it is," answered Dylan reassuringly, as she looked up into the face of her second son. She added to herself, *the only thing he seems to have stolen is my heart and the police can't help me get that back.*

"Who is he then, Mummy?" Danny wanted to know, coming to sit on the edge of his mother's bed, "How did he get here? Did he come when we were in bed?"

Dylan's mind was whirling. What explanation could she give to her children that would satisfy their growing curiosity? "Yes, he arrived last night, after you were all in bed."

"But who is he?" asked two small voices together.

Dylan said the first thing that came into her mind. Taking a deep breath, she said with her fingers crossed, "He's my cousin. He's from America. Now be quiet, or you'll wake him up."

"Can we go and see him now, Mummy?" asked Danny, heading for the spare room.

"We'll be real quiet, just like mice," Glen added, as he followed his brother up the hallway walking on tip toes in order to be extra quiet.

"No, boys, don't!" hissed Dylan as she flew out of bed trying to stop her children before they reached the spare room. She was too late and had no other option but to follow her sons into the room. Looking over at the bed, Dylan was horrified to see Adam was awake and looking at the three of them intently through green eyes that seemed to hold a devilish gleam in their depths. He'd obviously known this was coming and seemed to be ready for the questions she knew her children would ask.

Dylan on the other hand was at a complete loss. "Sorry about my children coming in. I tried to stop them, but they're naturally curious about you. How did you sleep?" She was unable to drag her eyes away from his body. His form was clearly outlined under the covers and was having a heady effect on her. His hands cradled his head, making his chest muscles bulge becomingly. *Oh, to be held in those strong arms.*

Adam smiled. Dylan already loved that smile. "They didn't wake me and I slept like a rock, cousin."

Dylan just stared at him, not knowing what to say. Her dilemma must have shown on her face because he said softly, "It's okay."

"Thanks. I'll explain later." Before anymore could be said between them, Danny and Glen walked over to the bed wanting to get a better look at this new grown up person who had suddenly turned up in their lives.

"Are you really mummy's cousin?" Danny wanted to know. With a child's determination he was going to find all the answers. Dylan didn't realise it, but he got this trait from her.

Adam hesitated before answering, then seeming to have made a decision, he stated, "I'm not really mommy's cousin, but we are friends. I turned up very late last night, so your mother said I could stay. Only a good friend would do that, wouldn't they?"

"Adam!" Dylan cried, wondering why he'd gone against her wishes.

Adam opened his mouth to speak, but was stopped short by Danny's next question. "Does this mean you and mummy are going to get married?"

"Danny!" Dylan exclaimed. She could feel the bright flush of embarrassment stain her cheeks. Adam's laughter rang around the room. It was a deep throaty laugh that had Dylan's senses reeling. Why wasn't he as embarrassed as she was?

"I was planning on getting to know you all a little better before I asked her that."

At this unexpected answer, Dylan's eyes flew to Adam's face. She thought she'd see someone who was laughing at her. She saw mirth in those sexy green eyes, but for a moment, she thought she saw something else. A fleeting expression so quickly veiled, she thought she must have imagined it; an expression of passion. Dylan sucked in her breath as she lowered her eyes, too confused to comment.

Undaunted, Danny pressed on. "Did you bring us any presents?" He looked expectantly around the room for anything that might remotely resemble a gift.

Glen seconded this question before Dylan was able to bring her sons to order. She was still shaken by Adam's earlier reply. Of course he'd been joking. It was probably his way of getting out of an embarrassing situation.

"Danny, Glen," Dylan admonished her sons sternly, but they weren't to be put off so easily.

"Well Nana always brings us presents when she's been away," Danny persisted, arguing his case.

"What's your name then?" questioned Glen, with the sort of tenacity only a four year old child could have.

"It's Adam. Adam Rossiter," he told them. He glanced over at Dylan who became aware of only having her nightgown on again.

Glen walked over to the edge of the bed and scrutinised Adam with a long, hard stare before saying to him, "You talk like Superman," He turned to his mother to ask her, "Is he Superman, Mummy?"

"No, Glen, he's not Superman." Dylan couldn't keep up with the barrage of questions that her children kept throwing at Adam. She couldn't even think of an appropriate answer to that one.

"Why?" Glen wanted to know.

"Superman and I come from the same place, Glen. We sound alike when we speak," Adam told him, by way of an explanation.

"Come on, boys, let Adam get dressed, or do you want to stay in bed a while longer?" she asked him, as she pushed her boys out of the room before her.

"No, I'll get up now," he told her, starting to move from under the covers.

"Um . . . I'll get us all some breakfast," Dylan told him making a hasty exit from the room. She turned back to ask, "Will bacon and eggs do?" He was looking at her in amusement.

"What?" Dylan asked, confused by his stare.

"Nothing," he answered, but his eyes said something else. Dylan thought she detected a look of what . . . could it have been tenderness? No, not this man, she was letting her emotions run away with her. He's just playing a game and I'm the pawn.

Trying to stop her children from asking questions while they ate was one thing, but Dylan couldn't keep them silent once they'd eaten their fill.

"How come we didn't know about you before, Uncle Adam?" Danny asked, as he came around the table to sit next to Adam. The uncle part had been added earlier, when the boys had wanted to know what they were going to call him. Dylan decided she'd stay out of this particular conversation. She sent him a look across the table that told him he was on his own.

Adam acknowledged her look with a lift of his eyebrows. His expressive eyes were telling her he'd take up the challenge she had given him. "Well, boys, your mother hasn't seen me in a long time, so I guess she forgot about me."

I couldn't forget about you if I tried, Dylan thought to herself.

"Have you ever been to Disneyland, Uncle Adam?" Glen wanted to know. To a four year old, this place was Mecca.

"Yes, I have. Actually, I was there just a little while ago, before I came over here," he told his captive audience.

"Wow, you lucky thing," the boys chorused and then started telling each other the things they'd do if they ever had the chance to visit Disneyland. Adam was momentarily forgotten as her two sons jumped up from the table, to make their way downstairs.

Looking out of the window, first at her children and then gazing up at the sky, she commented, "Anyway, it looks like the storm's gone. I guess that means we're in for another scorcher." Dylan knew she was rambling, talking a lot of nonsense, but she was unable to stop herself.

"You look like you take advantage of the sun whenever you can," Adam told her, glancing at her in a way that scorched her skin much more than the sun ever would. Her heart had started a tattoo and a delicious tingling had started to permeate throughout her body.

"I get outside with the kids whenever I can. It's not hard in this climate to get a tan," Dylan answered, looking at Adam's face. He was sporting a good tan himself. She assumed his job, whatever it was, took him out of doors quite a bit. She fought a strong urge to reach out and touch him. Getting up quickly from the table, trying to stem the way her thoughts were travelling, she knocked a cup of milk out of Natalie's hand. It catapulted across the table, landing all over the front of Adam's shirt.

"Oh, Adam, I'm so sorry," wailed Dylan, looking at the milk that had started to soak into his shirt.

Getting a strange gleam in his eyes, Adam slowly started to unbutton his shirt. He said with a devilish smile, "If you wanted to get my clothes off, I know an easier way to accomplish it. It's also much more enjoyable."

"Give it to me and I'll wash it for you. It will dry in no time," Dylan suggested, by way of a reply. She just wasn't up to these mind games with members of the opposite sex. She thought it was better to cut and run before she was in way over her head. Her nerves were stretched to breaking point. She almost wished Adam's ride would come and take him away.

"Dylan, come here," commanded Adam, when she rose from the table. She wanted to turn and run, but found herself doing as he asked, almost against her will.

"I want to kiss you. You're having a strange effect on me," Adam told her, by way of an explanation as he lowered his head, his lips meeting hers. The kiss was tentative at first, as if he was unsure of himself, but then he wrapped Dylan in his arms, while his probing tongue found its way into the sweetness of her mouth. Dylan returned his kiss, giving her turbulent emotions full reign. She was unable to stop herself. He had the power to make her forget all of her previous decisions about making love with someone on a casual basis. She moulded herself to him, pressing herself closer in a feverish attempt to satisfy her growing need of him.

Groaning with pent up desire and fighting to catch his breath, Adam whispered raggedly against her mouth, "Wow, lady, you sure know how to make a guy feel welcome!"

Nonplussed by these words and feeling like the wind had been knocked out of her, Dylan pulled back to stand passively within the circle of Adam's arms. Tears started to gather in her eyes and a few actually trickled down her cheeks unchecked. *What can I say to defend myself,* thought Dylan? *I've acted like a complete slut. He probably thinks he's onto a good thing, what man wouldn't after the wanton way I've been acting?*

Feeling the wetness of her tears on his bare chest, Adam stood back to survey her face. He frowned, wiping his thumbs gently under her eyes to clear away the traces of her tears, "Do you want to talk about it?" His tone suggested complete understanding, bringing a fresh wave of tears that threatened to put an end to any explaining Dylan might be prepared to offer.

"I feel . . . I mean we don't know each other and we've . . . I . . . I don't do this, I've never done this . . . acted like this with anyone else. I don't want you to think . . . ," this time Dylan couldn't continue. She desperately hoped he realised what it was she was trying, so badly, to impart to him.

"I'll let you into a little secret," his voice dropped down to a conspiratorial whisper, as he added, "I've never done anything like this before either, but you know something? If I thought the outcome was going to be the same, I wouldn't hesitate about doing it again as long as I knew you were the woman involved."

Seeing the sceptical look Dylan was appraising him with, he continued, his voice normal. "We need to talk. When I come back, and I mean to come back, Dylan, I'll tell you all about myself. I don't want to have to leave half way through my explanation if my ride turns up, just trust me, okay."

"Okay," Dylan agreed feeling a bit apprehensive and not really sure she was making the right decision, but she felt better knowing the matter was out of her hands.

"Good girl. Now where were we?" his face took on a look of concentration, as he conjured up a thoughtful expression, "Oh, yeah, I remember, we were here," he lowered his mouth to Dylan's, his arms pulling her closer, moulding her body to his.

A little while later saw them both outside. Dylan had the look of a woman who'd been thoroughly kissed. Her lips were red and a little bit swollen, there was a light in her eyes that had been absent for a very long time, if it had ever been there at all.

Adam had carried Natalie downstairs, and was in the act of putting her down next to the boys in the sand pit. A gesture they didn't appreciate.

"Uncle Adam, don't put her down here. She'll mess up the road we just made," protested Danny, scowling at his sister as she descended on them gleefully, her chubby little legs covering the short distance in a few seconds.

"No, she won't," Adam told them.

"Wanna bet," Dylan mumbled from the corner of her mouth to no one in particular as she sent a knowing smile towards her children and Adam as they sat talking in the sand pit.

Danny claimed Adam's attention before he could answer her quip, but he sent her an inquiring look that scorched her skin to the very roots of her hair. "When are you going, Uncle Adam? Why can't you stay with us for a while?" Danny abandoned his efforts to keep Natalie out of the way and had come to stand beside Adam. He continued, "If you don't like your bed, mummy will let you sleep in with her like she does with Glen and me. Mummy has lots of room in her bed."

Dylan felt the colour instantly redden her cheeks at the remark her son had so innocently made. When she finally had the courage to look at Adam, she could see he was valiantly trying to keep a straight face. He looked at Danny, saying in a serious voice that held only the slightest trace of a tremor, "Thanks for the offer son, but I'd probably keep your mom awake all night . . . um, with my snoring," He continued, perfectly serious this time, "How about I come back in a few days' time and we'll talk about it?"

"Yes, please, Uncle Adam," squealed two voices in unison, before heading back to the sand pit. Dylan could hear them discussing the gifts they were going to ask Uncle Adam to bring back for them.

Once the boys were out of earshot and Adam had joined Dylan once more on the back steps he inquired politely, "Do you think he means for me to come back, or is he offering me your bed?"

Dylan felt herself caught up in the madness of the moment, so she told him in a voice that she tried to keep as bland as she could, "Oh, to be in with me, to be sure, but I'm here to tell you I've no wish to be kept awake all night with your snoring, Mister Rossiter, thank you very much."

Adam made a playful swipe at her. His hand connected with her rear end. He told her in a voice that held amusement, "You'll keep." The words held a wealth of meaning for them both.

Their conversation became general until Adam looked directly at Dylan to ask, "Have you been seeing anyone since you've been divorced?"

"No." Dylan announced somewhat shortly, then immediately felt contrite; after all it had been a fair question, "No," she said again, somewhat subdued, "who'd be interested in a woman with three young children? Not every man wants the responsibility of bringing up another man's kids as his own."

"Maybe so, but don't lump us all in together. There are some men who just might think kids would be extra icing on the cake. If I was interested in someone it wouldn't matter if she had a dozen kids, not if I loved her," upon saying this, he walked over to where Dylan's children were playing in the sandpit and promptly sat down with them. Dylan could hear him telling them what he thought was the best way to build a sand castle without it falling down.

He had definitely left her with a lot to think about. She was sure his last remark had been made to let her know that if they did enter into a relationship, he'd welcome her children. She argued the pro's and con's back and forth while she tried to reach a solution that she thought she could be happy with. Everything was happening so swiftly, yesterday life had been so uncomplicated and then a tornado called Adam had swept into her life, turning everything upside down in a matter of hours. But as was the case with all whirlwinds, they caused a lot of damage before travelling on to other places. The dilemma facing Dylan was whether to ride out the storm and face the odds which could quite possibly be stacked against her if Adam turned out to be just another male on the make, wanting only to add another scalp to his belt. Or should she batten down all of her hatches and play it safe until the storm had passed, and not risk losing her heart and soul to a man she virtually knew nothing about?

Presently he walked back over to where Dylan sat and held out his hand to her. She put her hand into his as if she'd been doing it all of her life. She'd made her decision.

Shortly afterwards, a car pulled up outside. The driver tooted the horn madly. Obviously whoever Adam's friends were, they had no intention of coming inside.

"Your chauffeur's here, Adam," Dylan observed, as she peered through the window, hating herself for trying to get a better look at the woman who was to take Adam out of her life. Hopefully, it was only a temporary separation; Dylan wanted this man to come back.

"Okay. Don't worry about the car. Someone is going to come and get it later on. I'll be back to see you, Dylan. We have some unfinished business, you and I." the meaningful look he gave her had Dylan's heart pumping madly and a delightful tingling had started all over her body, yet again.

As soon as Adam got into the car, it started moving away from the kerb. *He didn't look back or even wave,* thought Dylan, feeling suddenly depressed. The house felt strangely empty after Adam had gone, almost as empty as her heart.

"This is stupid," Dylan told herself, "How can a grown woman behave like this?"

Answering herself, she said, "Because you love him." No, her mind taunted her. You can't love him. That just isn't possible. Love at first sight is a myth conjured up by those silly romance writers, isn't it. It didn't happen to intelligent, rational people. No, there had to be another reason, but try as Dylan might to think of another reason why a certain pair of sexy green eyes, when they'd looked at her in that certain way, had the ability to completely disarm her senses she could think of nothing else, but loving Adam Rossiter.

Walking into the bedroom, Dylan studied her reflection in front of the mirror, twisting this way and that trying to see herself as others did. The face that looked back at her wasn't too bad she supposed. She ran her fingers over her lips, remembering the kisses she'd shared with Adam earlier that morning. *Heavens, had it only been a few hours since they'd shared their special magic.* Dylan felt as if a lifetime had passed since she'd gazed into Adam's incredibly sexy, green eyes. They were like deep pools and if Dylan wasn't careful, she knew she could quite easily drown in them.

A few hours later found Dylan outside, working in the garden. She'd decided pulling out weeds was as good a way as any to use up all of this extra energy she seemed to possess all of a sudden. Her mind put forth a suggestion that Dylan found she couldn't refute . . . *sexual frustration, my girl. You're feeling the tension of unfulfilled sexual release.*

She'd been hard at it for some time, when a tow truck pulled up outside the house. Dylan stood up, thinking the drivers might like something cool to drink. She watched as they expertly put the car onto the back of the truck, thinking once they'd done this they would come over to her. How wrong could one person be, not only did they not come over, but they added insult to injury when Dylan heard one man turn to his friend to say in a voice that she realised she was meant to hear, "Trust him to break down here. I wonder if he tried his famous love scene out on this one."

A myriad of emotions coursed through Dylan as those shattering words sank into her brain. She didn't understand what those cruel words were meant to imply until the second man replied laughingly, "Knowing Adam Finlayson, he didn't have to. When a bloke looks like he does, all he has to do is crook his little finger and the sheilas practically fall into bed with him. Wish I had his luck cause that one looks like a real goer."

Adam Finlayson. No, it couldn't be. Now she remembered where she'd seen him. How could she have been so stupid to not have recognised him? Dylan felt physically sick as she stood listening. Her face had lost every vestige of colour it possessed and had turned a pasty white. Her legs threatened to collapse from under her and it took every ounce of dignity she possessed, and then some to calmly turn and walk serenely inside as if she didn't have a care in the world. Once inside the safe boundary of her home, Dylan's resolute facade crumbled and she gave in to the anguish that threatened to overcome her. It seemed she should have listened to her mind instead of following her heart, after all.

Dylan's mind registered the departure of the truck which meant her tormentors had gone. That was how she perceived them, these men, who with their malice and uncaring words had brought Dylan's world crumbling down around her. Humiliating tears coursed down her cheeks, dropping unchecked into her lap as she sat staring miserably at the wall. No wonder Adam had seemed so familiar to her. He was just about the hottest thing to come out of Hollywood in the last ten years. She'd recently watched one of his movies. Remembering the vivid love scene she'd viewed made her face flame. She'd cried for him, for he had loved and lost. But unlike the movie where he'd only been playing a part, she'd put her heart into the kisses they'd shared. How he must be laughing at her. *To think I was gullible enough to believe him,* thought Dylan sadly. He wouldn't be back; it was all just an act for him, a very convincing one at that, but still just an act. Those men must have been Adam's way of letting her know, how else would they have known what had happened?

Well, I told you so, whispered a small voice from the back of her mind. She tried to console herself with the fact that he hadn't had the satisfaction of taking her to bed. At least she'd saved herself from that small bit of humiliation. She had no choice, but to forget him and to get on with her life.

Erasing her memory of this man wouldn't be an easy task. Love wasn't an easy emotion to get rid of. Dylan recalled their conversation from that very morning. He'd told her he'd explain everything the next time he saw her, he said he'd be back. He'd promised. A little spark of hope still burned in a darkened corner of Dylan's heart, refusing to be extinguished, willing her to go on believing in the man she loved.

Fool, her mind screamed, forcing her to again take cover behind the protective wall her injured heart had erected for itself once before, long ago. *What has to happen before you'll believe the evidence that's been placed before your very eyes? Would you have preferred the degradation of a one night stand, turning into the kind of woman you profess to loathe?* Dylan shuddered knowing the answer to that question already. Surely the self-respect she had for herself would allow her to come to her senses and forget this incident ever happened.

She tried unsuccessfully to forget Adam by throwing herself into her work. She was soon worn out physically, but not mentally. Her longing for Adam tormented her. Her nights were filled with dreams of him, where they'd make love, but every morning she'd wake up alone and frustrated with her hopes of hearing from him slowly fading.

To make matters worse, Jake had been hassling her, making her life very miserable indeed. At least her sons weren't at home to witness their father's degrading verbal attacks. School holidays had started a few days ago. Dylan's parents had taken the boys, telling her they thought she needed a break, but Dylan knew this was just a feeble excuse on their part. They loved to have the boys. Dylan had kept Natalie at home, telling her parents she'd need some company after work. She wished now that she'd let Natalie go with her brothers. Missing out on Jake's regular tongue lashings would have to be a definite plus in Dylan's opinion.

Her ex-husband had made several phone calls already this evening since Dylan had arrived home from work, telling her each time that he was on his way around to see her. The last thing she wanted, or needed, at the moment was a visit from Jake. Her temper was definitely frayed and her mood more than soured, when a knock sounded at the front door. Dylan thought it was Jake carrying out his threat of coming around to intimidate her. She'd had enough, so without even thinking to check who was standing there, Dylan exploded as she walked towards the door, venting her anger and frustration of the past two weeks on Jake. She started to tell him just what she thought of him and his childish antics. To her horror, it was Adam standing there. His green eyes were watching her in an amused way as she stopped short, her hand going to her mouth as she realised who her visitor actually was.

"Is this how you answer your door these days, Dylan?" he could see she was furious at someone, but he hadn't been able to resist asking just the same.

"Oh, it's you, is it? Slumming again are you, Mister Finlayson?" Dylan answered sarcastically adding as much venom to her voice as she could muster, unburdening more of her anger on the man who stood watching her. She had the pleasure of seeing him pale under his tan, but still her traitorous heart started beating faster at the sight of him.

"Will you stay quiet long enough to let me explain," Adam asked quietly, injecting a note of authority into his voice.

"Do I have any choice?" Dylan flung at him. She found just being near him was having a disastrous effect on her. She'd started trembling and had to steel her body to stop herself from reaching out to him.

"Just say the word and I'll leave," Adam stated, looking at her seriously. She was certainly upset about something other than finding out who he was and he meant to find out what was behind it all.

"I'm curious. Why did you come back?" she inquired, with a challenging lift of her chin, showing a tenacity she was far from feeling.

"I thought that would have been obvious," Adam replied. He wished now he'd taken the time to explain who he was to Dylan, but it would have spoilt things.

"The only reason that comes to mind is to try to get me into bed, but I would have thought that someone as famous as you are wouldn't have any trouble finding someone stupid enough to fall for your charms," Dylan injected all of the hurt of the last two weeks into her statement telling herself it was the right thing to do and hopefully it would appease her wounded spirit by letting him know what she was thinking.

"I don't think you really believe that. The woman I came to know the last time I was here wouldn't think that of anyone," he told her, studying her face looking for signs which would help him to work out the change in her attitude towards him.

"That was two weeks ago, Adam," Dylan retorted, using his name for the first time, "So I stand by my reasons that the obvious answer is you came back for what you didn't get last time."

Adam ignored the last part of Dylan's answer; his instincts told him he wasn't the cause of her initial burst of anger. "A lot has happened since I last saw you. For what it's worth, I've missed you," His gaze focused on her face to see how she digested this last piece of information.

Dylan looked at him intently and then to her utter embarrassment, she started to cry. She turned away so he wouldn't see the tears and began walking towards her bedroom.

Adam caught her before she'd gone two steps. He turned her around to gaze down into her tear stained face, before he asked softly, "Dylan, what's happened? Who did you think I was just now?"

"Jake," Dylan told him through her tears, "Every so often he comes around trying to make trouble. He won't leave me alone. I just want to be left alone."

Adam took a handkerchief from his pocket and started to wipe away the tears, but this gesture only seemed to make the tears flow faster.

"Oh, Adam, I've missed you, too," Dylan acknowledged through her tears. She turned her trembling body into him as the hurt of the past two weeks came tumbling out.

"Feel better now, Love?" Adam asked, as she stood passively within the circle of his strong arms.

"I'll be okay," she murmured, drawing comfort from the strength of him.

"Good, then I'm sure you won't mind if I do this," Adam said, as he took Dylan's face tenderly in his hands and then slowly brought his lips down to cover hers. He'd meant for the kiss to be one that would demonstrate to Dylan that he understood her misgivings about him, but like all good plans, this one, too, fell apart and was soon forgotten, because as soon as their lips met all of his good intentions fled and he found himself caught up in an all-consuming passion that threatened to explode around him.

Dylan felt it too. Her body shook from repressed passion, as they reluctantly pulled apart. They both knew this wasn't the time for their long awaited bonding to take place. There were still unanswered questions to be dealt with.

"I've wanted to do that for so long," Adam whispered. His voice was thick with passion. His eyes looked as if he was coming out of a dream.

Looking up at him, Dylan knew her own desires would be mirrored there for him to see, also. To hide them seemed silly. "Yes, I know what you mean," she whispered shakily, stepping back from him. Catching her breath, she told him apologetically, "I'm sorry about before. I was worked up over Jake and upset about some other things. I guess I took everything out on you."

"Those other things wouldn't be me by any chance?" Adam asked soberly. He could have kicked himself for not having the sense to have phoned her. It would have saved a lot of hurt on Dylan's part had he done so.

Dylan shrugged her shoulders, not wanting to commit herself to answering any of his questions at this time. After all, she still didn't know why he hadn't been in touch. They'd moved to the kitchen where she was making them a much needed cup of coffee.

"Where is everyone by the way?" Adam asked, looking through the window, expecting to see the boys and Natalie playing outside.

"The boys are with mum and dad. Actually, I'm supposed to pick them up tomorrow. Natalie's in her room, she went to sleep when we arrived home." Her little daughter had been exhausted after a day out with Rae and Tom.

Adam's "Oh." held a wealth of meaning for Dylan, but she chose to ignore the implication and said nothing. She chose instead to put her coffee cup to her lips. If Adam noticed her trembling hand, he kept it to himself. They seated themselves at the kitchen table, with the table acting as a barrier between them, while Adam tried to make Dylan understand why he'd withheld his true identity from her.

"When you make movies like I do and have been fairly successful, you think twice about telling anyone who you are. Most women, when they know who I am, fall all over themselves to get at me. After a while you get sick of it. Dylan, please don't laugh. I'm serious. Anyway, when I came here that night and you didn't seem to recognise me, I didn't see any point in saying anything that first night, because I thought I'd be going away, never to see you again. I enjoyed being me . . . just plain Adam Rossiter. Rossiter is my correct surname by the way. It was only later, when I knew I cared for you that I knew I had a problem with not telling you. How did you find out anyway?"

Dylan told him word for word what the two men had said. She had the satisfaction of seeing the anger building on his face. "Those bastards! Wait until I get my hands on them. They'll be out on their ears."

"No, Adam, please, it's alright, it's not important anymore," Dylan reached out to take his hand wanting to reassure him that she understood his reasons for not telling her who he was.

Adam took the hand Dylan offered. He caressed her palm with the ball of his thumb, as he said, "Whose crummy idea was it to sit like this . . . oh, yeah, I remember . . . mine," he reminded himself, as he rose still holding her hand. He walked around to where Dylan sat to gently pull her to her feet. He raised her hand to his mouth and softly kissed her palm, saying as he did so, "I'm the one who should be saying I'm sorry. Can you ever forgive me for being such a jerk?"

"Yes," Dylan said simply, but added, "You can tell me more later."

He looked relieved, as he said to her, "We'd be much more comfortable sitting on the lounge, you know."

"Really," Dylan stated blandly, as she fought to keep the smile from her face. He was being completely transparent in his actions, as he led her across the room. Dylan lapped it up. A bit of honest, flirtatious fun was just what she needed to help her heal a very badly bruised heart.

Adam stopped to kiss her, running the tip of his tongue across her lips as he did so. This small action sent tiny, erotic tingles racing up Dylan's spine and she shuddered ecstatically, as her body responded to him. Taking a small step towards him brought her into contact with his body. Her breasts brushed softly against him, but it was enough to have her senses reeling. She felt him swell against her and took pleasure in the fact that he was consumed by the same longing that was overtaking her. The next few minutes were spent in ignorant bliss of their surroundings, as they took their fill of each other. Their minds were empty, except for the skyrockets that seemed to be exploding with a chaotic brilliance, blinding them to everything else but their urgent need for each other.

The loud thumping on the front door caused them to pull apart and resting their foreheads intimately together, they both tried to bring a sense of normalcy back to their ragged breathing.

"Someone's got lousy timing," Adam muttered, when he could finally speak.

"I'll second that," Dylan agreed, as she started for the door only to stop short when she saw who was there, the abrupt stop caused

Adam to cannon into her so that he had to hold onto her shoulders to steady himself.

"Jake!" Dylan had completely forgotten about her ex-husband and his threats. The shock of seeing him made her voice sharper than she'd intended it to be. The man standing before her flinched and then paled as he took in the scene before him. He was tall, almost as tall as Adam and where Adam's hair was light brown, Jake's was darker with a slight curl to it. He was a handsome man, but his features at the moment showed definite signs of anger.

He said to the couple standing before him in as insolent a manner as he could muster, "So I finally get to meet the boyfriend? You could have picked one with more guts, Dylan. Does he always hide behind your skirts?" Adam's hand tightened on Dylan's shoulder, but he restrained himself from taking any action.

"It's not what you think, Jake. I've told you time and time again there's been nobody else, not that it's any of your business anymore. We are divorced," Dylan threw at him, looking at the man she had once loved.

"You heard the lady, pal, she wants you to leave," Adam stated, side stepping around Dylan to stand in front of her.

"Who's going to make me?" Jake questioned, stepping through the door into the living room where he proceeded to make himself comfortable in one of the lounge chairs.

"Dylan, why don't you go and check on Natalie? I think Jake and I should have a talk," Adam gently pushed a protesting Dylan up the hallway that led to the bedrooms, letting her know with his expressive eyes that everything would be alright. He told her to shut the door.

Sometime later, Dylan heard the roar of an engine which was followed by the screech of tyres as a car tore away from the kerb and raced down the street. Moments later, Adam knocked on the door and not waiting for an answer, he let himself in. Dylan gazed up at him not knowing what to expect. Adam just smiled, telling her simply, "You can come out now, he's gone."

"What happened? What did you say to each other?" She was puzzled by his behaviour.

"We sorted out a few things, nothing to worry about," Adam replied nonchalantly.

"But . . . ," was all Dylan was able to get out before Adam put a finger over her lips, telling her to trust him.

"He won't hurt you anymore," he added, as he looked around the room as if he was looking for something, "Where's Nat's cot?" he wanted to know.

"She's in her own room now," Dylan told him simply, while looking at the vacant spot where her daughter's cot had stood for the last two years.

"Where do you put your visitors now?" he asked idly, directing his steady gaze at her.

"I haven't had anyone here who I've wanted to ask to stay," Dylan replied, finding her breath was catching in her throat as she looked up at him.

"Until now?" Adam questioned, watching her intently.

"Until now," she repeated, completely mesmerised by a pair of soft green eyes that seemed to be holding her captive in their sexy grasp.

"Come here," Adam asked, holding his arms out to her. Dylan happily moved into the circle of his arms, content to stay there and be held securely by the man she loved.

"Mummy, where are you?" they heard a small voice call out.

"In the bedroom, Honey," Dylan answered her daughter's inquiry.

As Natalie rounded the corner, she saw her mother being held in Adam's arms. She stopped dead in her tracks, uncertainty showing on her young face.

"Hello, Natalie," Adam spoke softly to the little girl, but didn't make a move to approach her in any way.

Natalie made her way to her mother's side from where she continued to observe Adam. When recognition dawned on her as to who he was, she gave him a small smile, but didn't attempt to go any closer.

Dylan knew they'd have to postpone any talking they had to do until later that night when Natalie was once again in bed. She wondered glumly if they'd ever get the chance to be together without being interrupted, so far things didn't look very promising. Looking across at Adam, she hoped he understood. She was a mother and she couldn't, or more to the point, wouldn't push her children aside for any man, not even this one. It would be better to end it now before she was too badly hurt. The thought of giving him up before they'd made love saddened her, but that's how it would have to be.

"Things aren't exactly working out as you planned they would, are they? First an angry ex-husband and now a demanding little girl; If you want to cut and run I'll understand," Dylan told him. She thought she was doing the right thing by offering him a way out.

The look Adam gave her wasn't exactly withering, but Dylan felt well and truly chastened by its intensity.

"There's no need to be like that. I had to ask, to at least offer you a means of escape," Dylan told him.

"I knew what I was getting into when I came back, Dylan. Not all men regard children as a chain around their necks. As for the other things, we've got all night," He pulled Dylan to her feet, kissing the tip of her nose as he did so, "I'm a big boy, I can wait."

When he would have turned to leave the room, Dylan grabbed his arm, forcing him to turn around. He looked at her inquiringly, waiting for her to speak. He saw the emotions flit across her face as she tried to put into words what she was feeling. "Thank you," she finally told him simply.

He just smiled before saying easily, "You're welcome." Before adding, "How about I go and get us some Chinese? I noticed a place as I drove down. Do you like Chinese?" He took hold of Dylan's hand and together they walked out of the room.

The mention of food made Dylan realise how long it had been since her last decent meal. She'd fallen into the habit of just picking at her food and then it had only been now and again.

"Yum, I love it. That sounds wonderful. I'll give Natalie a bath while you're gone." She had a quick shower herself, dabbing her pulse points with a perfume that she was particularly fond of. She pottered around the place not being able to sit still, picking up objects here and there only to put them back down again, breathing a sigh of relief when she heard Adam's car pull into the driveway. Walking out to meet him holding Natalie in her arms, she wasn't to know what a lovely picture she made standing there with the last feeble rays of the sun striking her hair giving it golden highlights. Natalie started to wriggle in her arms, trying to get down, so Dylan let her have her way. She ran to Adam, holding out her chubby little arms, wanting him to pick her up.

"Hang on a minute, Nat. Can you grab this food please, Dylan?" Adam responded warmly to the little girl, who was at this moment, pulling on his jeans letting him know in no uncertain terms that she was waiting for him to pick her up. He had a silly grin plastered on his face as he bent down to scoop the little girl up into his arms. He then swung her up onto his shoulders making her laugh gleefully as he did so. Dylan couldn't remember the last time she'd heard one of her children being so spontaneous and full of fun with anyone but herself or her immediate family. Her heart went out to this man all over again, thanking him silently for her daughter's laughter.

"I've never known Natalie to take to anyone so quickly before. She usually reserves judgment for a while," the child was sitting on Adam's lap while Dylan set the table for dinner. Adam had brought chopsticks, but Dylan set cutlery for herself, not knowing how to manage the wooden utensils.

"She's just got good taste like her mother. Do you want to change places with her?" Adam asked her. He was bumping Natalie up and down on his leg which caused the little girl to laugh anew, demanding more when Adam stopped.

"No . . . yes . . . not now. Ask me later." Dylan stammered feeling a slight blush creep up into her cheeks.

Adam grinned at her obvious dilemma, telling her he would.

Over dinner they indulged in small talk, but Dylan was finding it hard to concentrate and found she was fidgeting all the while. Adam was trying to teach her how to eat with chopsticks, but gave up after a while telling her she'd better stick to a fork for the time being. If he noticed her jittery behaviour, he said nothing about it. Dylan equated her behaviour to be like that of a bride on her wedding night. She felt nervous and was relieved when their meal was finished.

After the dishes had been done, Dylan had washed while Adam dried; she thought how natural he looked in these domestic surroundings. Sensing her train of thought, he said to her, "My sister's a widow. I spend a lot of my free time with her. She has two kids."

"Oh," Dylan didn't know what else to say to this bit of news about his family. It seemed odd to her that a big star like Adam Finlayson would do mundane things like wash and wipe dishes or do normal things the same as everyone else. She had always thought that people like him would live life in the fast lane going to endless parties and such like. "What about girl friends? You must have plenty of them hanging around," Dylan was surprised at the jealousy she felt when she thought of him having known other women.

"Not really. I try to stay away from the Hollywood parties as much as possible. I don't like to be used in all the wheeling and dealing that goes on. I leave that part of my career to my agent. I'm just an ordinary guy, Dylan, who happens to make movies. I'm one of the lucky ones. I was lucky enough to make it."

"Does that happen a lot?" At his questioning look she added, "The parties?" Dylan was starting to realise just how different their worlds really were.

"Pretty much," then changing the subject, he asked Dylan if she'd done the paintings that adorned her walls.

"No, my mother did most of them. They're good, aren't they?" Dylan was proud of her mother's talent. She followed Adam over to where he stood looking at one particular canvas.

"I like this one," Adam told her, taking a closer look. The painting depicted the harsh Australian outback where water was scarce and neighbours were few and far between. A decrepit squatter's shack made out of iron bark was in the foreground nestled amongst some tall gum trees. Dylan's mother had painted a broken fence that stretched for miles before it finally disappeared over the horizon. The loneliness seemed to reach out and grab you, trying to pull you in. The sky was a clear cloudless blue and a strong sun shone down onto a parched dry land that hadn't known the touch of rain for many years.

"Yes, its good isn't it. Mum has a special talent when it comes to painting." Dylan told him looking with fresh eyes at the art work that decorated her wall.

"Am I going to meet your parents, Dylan?" Adam asked out of the blue as he turned away from the paintings, pinning her to the spot with his green eyed stare.

"If you want to," she told him simply.

"I want to. I want to know everything about you, but I guess I owe you some answers as well. Natalie looks ready for bed. Why don't you get her ready and I'll open the wine," he suggested as he gestured towards the little girl who sat on the lounge. Her eyelids were drooping and her head was lolling onto her chest. She was almost asleep.

Chapter Three

Before long, they were seated on the lounge, their wine glasses standing on an occasional table in front of them. Adam was speaking, his deep voice holding a strange fascination for Dylan. The wine had calmed her down a little and she was having difficulty in concentrating on his actual words. Her mind seemed to be more interested in knowing when he was going to kiss her again. It took a moment before she realised Adam had stopped talking and was watching her. He had a strange expression plastered on his face.

"Dylan, you didn't hear a single word I said, did you? You were miles away. What were you thinking about, I wonder?" Adam queried softly as he brought his hand up to gently stroke her cheek, using his long fingers to trace a seductive path from her left temple to the side of her mouth.

Dylan could feel her skin burning as she looked at him. Her thoughts must have given her away because he groaned, then pulled her roughly to himself burying his head into the softness of her neck to start kissing her hungrily. His mouth drifted across to her ear where he bestowed light kisses over her lobe making her squirm in his arms as a deep burning started deep within the core of her. He kissed his way slowly back to her mouth bringing his lips down on hers in a kiss that left her in little doubt that he wanted her as much as she wanted him. One of Adam's hands started a slow journey, sliding seductively down Dylan's throat until it reached the front of her blouse. He started to undo the buttons, kissing her passionately all the while, making her pulses hammer. It wasn't long before the offending garment had been removed and had been flung onto the floor.

Dylan abandoned all of her inhibitions as she gave herself willingly to this man, showering kisses over his face and neck, nuzzling his ear with her lips. She pushed herself closer to him, loving the feel of his body next to her own. His touch tantalised her breasts and she could feel them becoming erect as her passion grew. She pulled at Adam's shirt, needing to feel his strong body next to hers.

"Dylan . . . Honey, be sure this is what you want. I don't know if I'll be able to stop if we go much further," His voice sounded heavy and was ragged and thick with emotion coming in short bursts as if he was fighting for every breath he took.

"I'm sure," Dylan answered raggedly. She was fighting to catch her breath too, but it was a beautiful sensation. She stopped her onslaught of him only long enough to whisper those two words before taking possession of his lips again, having felt deprived without them covering her own.

Finally rid of their clothing, their hands had the freedom to roam as they learnt about each other. Adam kissed her breasts, teasing her taut nipples out with his teeth. "You're beautiful," he told her brokenly, as he gazed down at her before gently forcing her back against the length of the lounge chair. Dylan gloried in his expert touch. His fingers blazed a scorching trail across her heated body; one that his lips followed at a more leisurely pace. He softly caressed her thighs before moving his fingers tenderly over the very core of her making her shudder violently against him as he continued to stroke her. She opened herself up to him oblivious to even having done so, so great was her need for him. She moaned against his lips, needing him to possess her. She wanted him to possess her. Her hands roved over his body. She played with his nipples and felt them grow erect, staying there only long enough to savour the maleness of them before she moved on. Her hands slowly made their way down across his stomach. She felt his stomach muscles flex as her fingers roamed over their firmness. She felt his intake of breath and a soft moan escaped his lips as she splayed her fingers around his belly before continuing their downward path to play with the soft hair that grew at the base of his manhood. Soon her hands had reached the object of her desire and she held him firmly, loving the feel of him within her grasp. She ran her fingers over and around him and was rewarded when she felt the wetness starting to seep from him.

"Oh . . . my . . . god, Dylan. Dylan, oh my god," he repeated as she continued to squeeze him giving him no mercy.

Moments later, Adam entered her with deep thrusting movements and Dylan welcomed him, arching her body towards him crying out in jubilation as they moved together, giving and accepting love one from the other. The explosive sensations they shared swamped them completely, until they reached the summit they'd been yearning for, falling headlong into a deep mindless chasm of turbulent, seething emotion.

Afterwards, lying sedately in Adam's arms, Dylan couldn't stop the tears from rolling down her cheeks. Concern filled Adam when he saw them. He asked, "Did I hurt you, Dylan? I tried not to, but you're so damn sexy, I lost control. I'm sorry."

"No, it's not that. You were wonderful," Dylan answered, wiping her eyes, "I was scared that if we ever made love, I'd let you down with you being who you are and all." She knew he would have had lots of women given who he was.

"Are you kidding?" he stated, lifting himself up on to one elbow, "You took me to places I've never been before and for god's sake will you stop throwing it up in my face about who I am. I'm just a guy who happens to think you're an incredibly sexy woman." He stooped to kiss her tenderly, before adding, "You're a very sensual woman, Dylan Miles. Hey, how did we get onto the floor?"

Dylan shrugged her shoulders, looking around her. They were stretched out on the carpet next to the sofa. She heard Adam starting to chuckle and wondering what he was finding so funny, followed his gaze across the room. She could feel her face starting to flame, as there amongst the foliage on one of the indoor plants sat her bra, hanging limply. *How did it get there,* she thought?

"I didn't think I'd ever see you blush again, after tonight. Don't ever change," Adam announced, smiling down at her. He thought how beautiful she looked laying here next to him with the soft glow of the lamp throwing alluring shadows over her naked body. His eyes roamed over her, coming to rest on her face. Finding her gaze on him, he simply held out his arms and Dylan went gladly into them, feeling safe and secure in his strong embrace. There followed a beautiful night of love, when they learned about each other's bodies, about the secret places only a lover can know.

Dylan awoke early the next morning to feel the unaccustomed weight of Adam's arm laying across her shoulder holding her protectively. She turned to watch the steady rise and fall of his chest as he slept, noticing the way the hair on his chest tapered down below his navel.

Kissing him tenderly on the cheek, Dylan felt the roughness of the stubble on his face, as slowly, waking from sleep he moved his lips towards her, kissing her gently on the lips.

"Dylan, I'm exhausted. Go back to sleep. You've had me awake all night," He mumbled something about being a sex slave, before he closed his eyes again, the satisfied grin not quite absent from his handsome features.

"I've had you awake all night!" Dylan exclaimed mockingly. Her mind went back over the events of the night when they'd made love without restraint. Her body felt alive and glowing. Her mind felt as if all of the cobwebs had been blown away.

During the night, they'd gone into the bedroom, and now Dylan tried to get up only to have Adam's arm snake out from under the covers to pull her back in next to him. He bit her playfully along the shoulder until he reached her breast. He teased her until she cried out for mercy, laughingly telling him she was sorry. He silenced her with a kiss that left her breathless. All thoughts of getting up had magically vanished from her mind as they savoured the closeness of each other.

Sometime later, easing himself up from the bed, Adam walked into the bathroom where Dylan had just turned on the shower taps, ready to step under the warm spray. He seemed perfectly at ease with his nudity. He had a beautiful body, with not an ounce of spare flesh. It gave Dylan pleasure to feast her eyes on him, knowing for the moment that he was hers.

"Dylan," Adam detained her, as she was about to step under the jets of water. He whispered, "Any regrets?"

"No, none," she countered softly, smiling up at him, "None at all."

Later in the day, they were sitting together on the back steps watching Natalie play. Adam had Dylan in stitches telling her some of the funny things that sometimes happened on the sets of the movies he'd worked on. He'd gone on to tell her that like most actors he liked to look at the rushes at the end of a day's shooting explaining that rushes was the term used for the work that was filmed on any particular day. It helped him to evaluate his performance.

"You have to leave you behind and become this character that looks like you sometimes, but is completely alien to you in every way. You have to be sensitive to your character's feelings regardless of his personality. You have to reinvent yourself; to find ways to become this other person that you have to create in order to make him believable."

They were interrupted by a knock at the door. Getting up to see who had caused this untimely intrusion, Dylan was dismayed to see Jo standing there.

"Hello, Jo. Come on in," Dylan announced, indicating that her neighbour should follow her to the back of the house where she made the introductions.

"Danny told my boys you pretended to be cousins. Now why would you do that, I wonder?" Jo laughed innocently, but there was a wealth of meaning behind those quietly spoken words.

"We didn't, not really. It was a joke," Dylan answered, smiling at Jo. Adam could see the smile didn't quite reach her eyes.

Jo quizzed Adam about a number of things before she finally rose to leave. She whispered to Dylan before she left, "Cousin or not, Dylan, try not to let this one slip through your fingers."

"What a nerve!" Dylan fumed as she shut the door after her neighbour had gone, "did you hear the things that woman said?"

"Calm down, Honey. This world is full of people like Jo. The trick is not to let them upset you," Adam told her. He was ticked off at the woman as well, but Dylan seemed to be angry enough for both of them.

"Darn it, Adam, doesn't anything ruffle that calm exterior of yours?" she flung at him, but was instantly sorry for her outburst, "Oh, I'm sorry. It's not your fault I have a nosy neighbour. I guess you're right though, but ooh, the nerve of some people," Dylan bristled again, storming back into the kitchen.

"I guess there's only one way to calm you down," Adam sighed. He walked across to her and using his body as a weapon pinned her against the side of the kitchen bench and without further comment, he started kissing her. At first his hands rested casually on the bench either side of her, but as their kiss deepened he brought his arms up to encircle her lovingly.

"I thought you wanted to calm me down," Dylan murmured against his lips before she, too, was lost in rapturous bliss.

"Mummy, I'm hungry," Dylan was brought back to earth when she felt a slight tugging on her blouse. She reluctantly lifted her lips from Adam's to glance down at her daughter.

"All right, Sweetheart," she sighed and would have moved away from Adam, but he barred her way. She looked up at him questioningly.

His eyes glinted mischievously with pure devilment. "Mommy, I'm hungry, too."

"You, sir, will have to wait your turn," she told him frivolously, all signs of her crankiness gone.

"Alas, my good woman, man cannot live by bread alone," he cried melodramatically, his hand slung casually across his heart.

Dylan couldn't help but laugh. She shot him a cheeky glance, as she responded to his bantering, "You know with a bit of practice you could develop into a dirty old man. I thought last night would at least see you through till tonight."

"That, my dear was just an appetiser," he winked, as he made a playful lunge for her, cornering her by the refrigerator where she had started to get the ingredients for Natalie's lunch, "Mm, now I've got you here, what am I going to do with you?"

Dylan feigned a look of complete innocence as she looked blankly at him. Already the stupid prank was forming in her mind, "Well, if you don't know, far be it from me to tell you."

She deftly swung out of his grasp, opening the refrigerator door a bit wider as she did so. Catching him off guard, she quickly pushed him towards the coolness, saying flippantly, "I was going to suggest a cold shower but now I . . . ," she got no further as two things happened simultaneously. Adam lost his footing and actually started falling into the fridge, knocking over the bottle of wine they'd opened the night before. The cork dislodged with a loud bang, flying through the air hitting the wall just above Dylan's head, causing her to jump with fright into Adam who immediately fell backwards into the fridge, taking her with him.

For a moment, Adam just sat there regarding Dylan intently. She couldn't read the expression on his face. *I think I've gone too far this time,* she thought as she started to back away, fearing retribution.

Adam lifted himself up gingerly, not taking his eyes from Dylan's face. He carefully felt behind himself, bringing his hand down to his backside. He brought out a piece of toast left over from breakfast that had stuck to his pants when he'd overbalanced.

"Adam, I'm sorry. It was only a joke. I didn't mean for any of this to happen," Dylan confessed, waving her arms around the room to take in the mess.

"My dear Dylan, if you wanted me on toast all you had to do was ask. And I thought I was the kinky one," the look he directed at her was full of laughter as he took in the relieved look on her face. Licking his fingers, he made for the door then turned back suddenly to tell her, "Mao's better."

When he was out of earshot, Dylan looked down at Natalie who had stood patiently waiting the whole time and told her simply, "When you fall in love, Sweetheart, make sure it's with someone like Adam."

Dylan put Natalie down for her afternoon nap before she and Adam were able to resume any serious conversation. He still hadn't told her anything about his two week absence. "Do you remember asking me if I was married, or whether I had a family back home and I said no?"

Dylan felt a cold sweat break out all over her body. She knew she'd paled. She tried to prepare herself for the words she thought she was going to hear.

"Yes," she whispered hoarsely, trying to withdraw her hands from his clasp, but found them held firmly within his strong grasp. She was amazed at how calm she sounded when inside her head she was screaming like a caged animal wanting its freedom.

"I've been married before, too. It's been over for years now, totally dead and buried. She remarried soon after our divorce. I've got a daughter, Dylan, she's ten. Her name is Teresa," Adam was looking closely at Dylan to see how she was reacting to his story so far.

"Go on," she prompted, interested despite herself.

"We were both young, but by the time we realised our relationship wasn't going to work, Erica found out she was pregnant, so we tried to make a go of it. I was away a lot, trying to establish my career. I came home unexpectedly one time and found Erica in bed with some guy. I walked out and never went back. That was ten years ago. Erica ended up marrying the guy later on. She didn't want me to see Terri, said it would only upset her with me popping in and out of her life, so I stayed away for Terri's sake," He stopped talking and gazed unseeing out of the window. Dylan could see he'd paled under his tan; no doubt this conversation had brought all the hurt back to haunt him.

"Anyway," he continued, "when I got back to my hotel after staying here that night, there was a phone call for me to call home.

It seems Erica and her husband had been to a party. On the way home, they were killed in a freak car accident. Terri was by herself. Erica's parents are dead. I was out of the country. They put her into a home until they could find me," He stopped, putting his arms around Dylan, holding her close. She could hear the torment in his voice, "I caught the first available flight home. She couldn't remember me, at all. We spent the next few days getting to know each other. She's at home with my parents. I thought it best not to bring her, she's had enough changes in her life for now," he finished at last, his voice curiously husky.

Dylan could feel the tears brimming behind her lashes as she fought for control, "Oh Adam," was all she could get past the lump in her throat. She looked at him through eyes that were bright with unshed tears. His own eyes mirrored hers in their brightness. It seemed natural for them to kiss, both seeking comfort one from the other, for the recent hurts they'd suffered.

Drawing away reluctantly, Dylan asked him if Terri had adjusted to her new situation.

"Yes, she's fine. My folks are great with her. She'll move in with me when I go home. Actually, I was thinking of getting a larger place. I know I should probably keep my mouth shut and give you more time to think about this, but I want you to come back with me, Dylan, or at least to follow shortly afterwards. Please say you'll at least think about it and give it some serious thought."

Dylan felt like she'd been waiting all of her life to hear those words. She wanted so badly to say yes, but Adam had never said he loved her in the time they'd been together. Dylan knew she loved him, but was that enough?

"Adam, I need to be sure. Jake and I . . . we . . . I loved him once and look at us now. I won't mistake sex for love. What I feel for you is different from anything I've ever experienced but . . . ," she got no further with her explanation because Adam interrupted her, to exclaim hotly.

"How can you call what happened here last night just sex! It meant more than a quick tumble in the hay to me. I thought what we shared was very special, didn't you?"

"Yes, yes it was, it was wonderful, but I don't want to make the same mistakes. There are more people to hurt than just you or I. I won't drag my children through any sordid affairs," she finished with a spurt of anger, wanting so badly for him to understand her motives.

"A sordid affair!" Adam exclaimed, jumping up to start pacing around the room, anger was evident in his every movement, "Dammit, Dylan, I just asked you to marry me and you accuse me of wanting an affair. I've had my fill of affairs and the nothingness they have to offer. I want a home, a family, a wife . . . I want you. Don't you realise that?" He stopped abruptly in front of her and pulling her to her feet he told her quietly in a voice that was filled with the emotion he was feeling, "I intend to make you love me, you know."

"I love you already," Dylan confessed. Her mind pleaded with him to say the same words to her, but they weren't forthcoming.

Instead he said, "That's a good start. Now tell me you'll come with me and be my wife." In spite of his brashness, Dylan detected a note of uncertainty, as looking up into his face she saw his handsome features were drawn and grim, as he waited for her reply.

There didn't seem to be any choice as far as Dylan was concerned. She loved this man. She'd been given a taste of how life would be without him. She didn't want to endure that pain again. It seemed like the decision had been taken out of her hands.

"I'll come with you," she said simply. Surely he'd tell her now how much he loved her. She needed to know. An awful thought struck her, what if he only wanted a mother for his daughter, a stable home life for her after her terrible ordeal. She'd be perfect for the role, already having children of her own. He'd said he was sick and tired of meaningless affairs so this could be his way of solving all of his problems.

The smile that he sent her had Dylan's heart racing. "Wait right here," he told her as he pushed her gently down onto the lounge chair before heading off down the short hallway towards the bedroom. He returned a few minutes later with a small parcel which he handed to her, telling her smilingly, "I got something for you when I went home. I hope you like it."

"Adam, you shouldn't have," Dylan felt elated that he'd thought of her at such a low point in his life. She opened the package with trembling fingers wondering what it could be. She found she didn't care; she was thrilled to have a gift of any sort from him.

Adam watched her as she investigated the gift he'd given her. He was sure she'd love it, if only she'd open it up completely.

Dylan thought Adam had given her a jewellery box. It was certainly beautiful. Her fingers roved gently over the smooth ebony black lacquered surface before tracing the outline of two beautiful ruby red roses that were inlaid into the centre of the lid. The roses were surrounded by delicate pale green leaves. The box was delicate as well, only being about four inches by six inches in size and about two inches deep.

"Adam, it's beautiful," Dylan told him softly as she gazed up at him. She could feel the emotion rising up from her throat as she looked back down at the gift that Adam had given her. "It's simply beautiful. I've never seen anything like it before."

"Why don't you open it," he told her simply.

"Yes, of course," she told him as she slowly lifted the lid. She thought she'd find a piece of jewellery lying within the confines of the box and indeed there was a beautiful gold linked bracelet lying in the small cubicle, but it was the music she started to hear that had her catching her breath. Adam had given her a music box, but no ordinary musical box if Dylan was any judge. The song that filled her ears was one she knew. Adam had had "Miss You Nights" by Dobie Gray implanted into the musical notes of the box. Dobie Gray's voice was filling the room with a clear, sweet sound that was pitch perfect. Most music boxes Dylan had listened to in the past seemed to produce a sound that was a trifle tinny, but the song she was hearing was as clear as if she was listening to it on the radio.

"Adam. Oh, my god, it's absolutely beautiful. I love it. Where did you get it?" Dylan's eyes had filled with tears of gratitude as she gazed up into the face of the man she loved. To give her a gift such as this was more than she could comprehend. She'd never seen anything like it. She knew that it would always be one of her most treasured possessions.

"It's from a place called the Music Box Attic in North Hollywood. A guy called Boris runs the place. He's a good guy. He goes out of his way to help if he can. Anyway, they make musical boxes to order and have all sorts of songs to choose from. Hundreds of the damn things, but lucky for me they had the song I was after, but if they hadn't Boris would have found it for me and inserted it into this box. They have all kinds of boxes, heart shapes and ballerinas as well as more of these, all sorts, all kinds of decorations too, but I liked this one. I hoped you'd like it as well," Adam told her, happy that she had liked his gift to her. He added, "I missed you while I was gone, and I'm sure I'll miss you all the more every time I have to leave you. I just wanted a special way to tell you, that's all."

"Oh Adam. I missed you to . . . so much. It's a perfect reminder and I'm sure I'll wear it out playing it when you're not here. I love it. No one has ever given me anything like this . . . ever," It was exquisite. Dylan carefully laid the box aside as the last strains of the song finished playing . . . *these miss you nights are the longest* . . . and rose from her chair to gather Adam into her arms. She gave him a giant bear hug, telling him through a fine mist of tears, "Thank you so much, Adam. I don't know what to say."

"Well, you know what they say," he told her somewhat glibly.

"No, what do they say?" she wanted to know smiling sweetly up into his face.

"They say that when words fail you . . . insert kisses instead." He had an inquiring look plastered over his handsome features knowing Dylan saw through his flimsy excuse to kiss her.

"Really. Do they now," Dylan was thoroughly enjoying the banter that was taking place between them, "Well, far be it from me to break with tradition." She offered her lips to him. She was more than ready to play this particular game of seduction knowing exactly where it would take her. She was impatient for the adventure to begin.

When Natalie woke up, they headed for the beach for what remained of the afternoon. The beach was deserted when they arrived and Natalie was happy to sit at the water's edge and have the waves lap gently over her. Adam was spread out on a towel, his eyes were closed and Dylan thought he'd fallen asleep. She studied him. She wanted to reach out and touch him, but she didn't want to wake him. She contented herself with just looking for now. Everything about him was perfect, his straight nose, his ears, his mouth set as it was in the shape of a sexy cupid's bow, everything. He had the longest eyelashes she'd ever seen on a man, not that they detracted from his masculinity in any way. She found herself wondering whether he might have had plastic surgery done to look this good. She'd heard a good many actors had surgery done to improve their looks, not that she thought Adam had, but still it wouldn't hurt to have a closer look.

Dylan edged closer to him on all fours, before crouching down next to his face. She was only inches away from his forehead, trying to see if she could detect any scars and had just about convinced herself that there weren't any, when one of his eyelids opened and a green eye looked up at her. His voice drawled softly, "Is this a one player game or can anyone join in?"

"Oh," Dylan jumped back in fright, "I thought you were asleep."

"Obviously, would you mind telling me what you were doing?" he'd turned onto his side and Dylan greedily ran her eyes down the length of him, savouring the sexy sight that was before her eyes.

"I was just looking," she told him defensively, feeling flustered by his knowing smile. *Damn, he looked good.* Dylan could feel her nipples becoming taut as her rampant thoughts led her astray. Flustered and embarrassed, Dylan realised that her imagination was running away with her. No wonder he was looking at her with such obvious enjoyment.

Adam reached out for her hand and placed it on his chest, "Looking's not much fun if you can't touch, as well."

Dylan loved the feel of him under her hand. She trailed her fingers slowly across his broad chest playing with his nipples. She had the pleasure of seeing them harden and become erect under her touch. On an impulse, she lowered her mouth to them, licking them in turn with her tongue. She started to suck gently while pulling at them provocatively with her teeth. She tasted his sweat, licking his chest as a cat would when cleaning her young. She knew Adam was enjoying her actions by the soft moans he emitted from time to time. He didn't make any move to touch her himself, he seemed content to let her play. Dylan's sexual appetite was being fed by her actions which had become quite seductive and provocative. She had moved her hand down to his groin and was softly massaging him through the fabric of his shorts. His response was immediate and his aroused state was clearly evident as Dylan looked hungrily down at him.

"Oh, god, Dylan, I think you'd better stop for a while or I'll have to take you right here on the sand," Adam croaked in a voice quite unlike his own. His hand reached out to cover hers in a firm grasp, "I don't think I can take much more. You're driving me crazy." He took a few deep breaths, trying to bring his ragged breathing under some semblance of control.

A few minutes later, he told her in a voice more like his own, "I think I'll go for a swim." He jumped up and began to sprint down the beach towards the water, where he dove cleanly between the waves before striking out for deeper water.

Dylan felt a strange exuberance knowing she was the cause of Adam's flight. It gave her womanly confidence a much needed boost; one it had badly needed. In fact, since knowing Adam, she'd blossomed from a shy, unworldly figure into this person who was still learning about the ways of the world. With Adam, all of her senses seemed to be heightened; he made her feel so vibrant and alive. She supposed that's what real love did to a person. She felt so alive, so electric. Every touch ignited nerve endings that set her whole body aflame.

She finally understood her decision to go with Adam, to risk everything, even breaking her heart if it didn't turn out the way she hoped. They shared a magic she knew she'd never find, or want, with any other man. If she couldn't share her life with him, she wouldn't seek anyone else. He'd be too hard an act to follow. She loved him completely.

Adam returned from his swim, grinning at her as he made his way back to where Dylan was sitting. She thought it best not to mention the reason for his going on a marathon swim.

"It's okay. You can gloat if you want to. I should have realised I couldn't remain passive once you started to touch me," he stated, looking down at her. His body glistened, still wet from the sea. Water ran down his chest making patterns through the hair that grew there.

"I don't want to gloat. I want to go home to finish what I started," she stated simply, gazing up at him, her eyes full of wanting. *Goodness, was this brazen woman really her? Had she just propositioned Adam? Well, as good as,* her mind told her.

"Come on, Love, let's go home," Adam gave a sigh of pure contentment as he pulled Dylan up into his arms. He held her closely before stepping back so he could look into her face. "You know I love you, don't you?" He made it sound like it had been a forgone conclusion.

"I know now," Words couldn't describe the euphoria Dylan felt upon hearing Adam say those words. They meant more to her than anything else he could have said or done.

Arriving home a short time later, Dylan had only taken a few steps towards the house when Adam's cry of alarm had her turning back to him. He seemed to be alright, although he had a strange look on his face. He was looking at Natalie. He held her in his arms, having taken her out of her car seat.

"Adam, are you alright? Are you sick?" Dylan quizzed him, while trying to take Natalie from his arms. There were so many things about him that Dylan didn't know. What if he was having a fit of some kind.

"I'm fine," he told her, putting her mind at rest.

"What then?" she questioned, thoroughly confused by his outburst. He definitely looked strange.

"Natalie has just wet on me," he told Dylan, trying to sound serious, but she could see the sides of his mouth starting to twitch as he gave in to the laughter he could no longer hold at bay.

"You, young lady, are no lady," He held the little girl away from him and then put her down gently beside him.

Dylan could see the tell-tale wet patch that had spread over his shirt and down the front of his shorts. She felt embarrassed over her daughter's lack of discipline. She was horrified when she started to laugh. She couldn't help it. She had to sit down on the steps, or she was sure she would have fallen. Tears of mirth gathered in her eyes and rolled down her cheeks before she was able to get herself under some semblance of control. Glancing at Adam, she saw he was in the process of removing his shirt, wanting to be rid of the offensive garment.

"Adam, I'm truly sorry. She's not fully toilet trained, but I never thought anything like this would ever happen," Dylan was in danger of starting to laugh again. She was having difficulty opening the front door due to the laughter she was trying so hard to suppress. In the end, she handed the key to Adam, stepping aside to give him access to the keyhole.

Stepping through the doorway, Adam responded, "I'll forgive her this time, but I'd hate it to become a habit," He was wiping himself with his shirt, wrinkling his nose in distaste when the smell reached his nostrils, "I'd better go and have a shower."

"I'll wash those clothes for you when you take them off," Dylan stated matter-of-factly. She had herself under control again and was able to respond to him sensibly, however, a streak of pure devilment made her ask him, "Do you still want that drink or do you think you've been wet enough for one day?" They'd decided on the way home to have a glass of wine before eating dinner.

The glance he directed at her as he walked from the room told Dylan he didn't think much of her sense of humour. Thinking she was safe to do so, Dylan poked her tongue at him only to be caught in the act, as he spun around. "Oops," she told him, by way of an apology.

Dylan could hear him singing in the shower. *It's a good thing he doesn't make his living as a singer,* she thought mischievously, or he'd be on skid row within a week. She put the finishing touches to their salads before putting them into the refrigerator. Adam re-entered the kitchen a short time later wearing a pair of hip hugging blue jeans and a darker blue cotton knit shirt. His hair was wet and he'd combed it back from his face. The overall picture was very appealing.

Sniffing the air, Dylan asked him would he mind sticking to this brand of after shave from now on as she had grave doubts about the other one he'd used. "Besides," she added, "the other one attracts flies. What did you call it again?"

"Ha, ha, very funny," Adam quipped, as he advanced towards her in a menacing way.

"What are you going to do?" queried Dylan warily as she started to back away as he approached her. She was stopped by a wall at her back that blocked her escape.

"Only this," Adam replied, putting a hand either side of her head as he brought his head down to hers in a kiss that left her breathless, but definitely wanting more of the same. When she'd have gone willingly into his arms, he held her at arm's length, nodding beside her to where Natalie stood watching them, "Don't you think Nat's a bit young to watch her mother in an 'R' rated performance?"

"I know that," Dylan lied. She knew he knew she'd lost her head. It was perplexing to completely lose your head over someone to the exclusion of everything else, even one's daughter, "I was just . . . just . . . ," she floundered, not being able to come up with a suitable excuse. She ran her tongue over her lips, looking at his mouth greedily, wanting more of him.

"Mmm, just what? I didn't catch that last bit," Adam teased her, obviously enjoying her discomfort. He cocked his ear towards her as if he hadn't heard her unspoken words. Pure devilry shone out of his eyes, as he gazed down at her.

"Just you wait, Adam Rossiter, that's what. I'll get you," Dylan challenged him gamely.

"I hope so," he returned smugly, "I certainly hope so."

Dylan had to concede defeat in this particular battle of wills and grudgingly told him so, adding as an afterthought, "But the game isn't over yet, Mate. This was just the first round."

"Okay," he smiled, pushing himself away from the wall where he'd been leaning. He winked at her before deliberately brushing against her breasts as he moved past her, causing Dylan to catch her breath as the now familiar fluttering started to erupt in the pit of her stomach.

Dylan felt pleasantly tired, as later that night she sat next to Adam on the lounge. Her head rested contentedly on his shoulder and her eyes were closed. Adam had helped put Natalie to bed and then he'd told the little girl a story until her eyelids had been too heavy for her to stay awake any longer.

They'd been listening to music while sharing a pleasurable lull in the conversation. "Dylan," she heard her name through a drowsy haze.

"Mmm?" was the best answer she could muster up from her drowsy state of mind.

"Do you think we could finish doing what we left this afternoon?"

Lifting her head from his shoulder Dylan turned to look at him. His eyes were soft and dreamy, his lips looked very inviting and she found herself being drawn towards them like a moth to a flame. Her tiredness had vanished to be replaced by her unquenchable desire for this man.

His tongue explored the soft contours of her mouth. There was an urgency in his movements as he pulled her towards him, laying her across his taut body. He'd denied himself all day, now it was his turn. Taking Dylan off guard, he picked her up in his capable arms and started walking towards the bedroom, where he put her gently on the bed, before coming to lay beside her himself. His kiss was slow and thorough as he expertly started to undo the buttons of her blouse. When the last button had been undone, he moved his fingers caressingly over her throat moving ever downwards towards her breasts, touching the flimsy piece of lacy lingerie she was wearing. Her nipples hardened in anticipation, as she waited for Adam's touch. In one deft movement the offending piece of underwear was gone. In its place, Adam's thumb and forefinger played first with one pink nub and then the other, making Dylan writhe with uncontrolled passion as his lips blazed a trail from her mouth down over her throat to slowly make his way to her breasts where he skilfully ran his tongue around her ripe nipples. The desire flooding her was so exquisite, it was almost painful. Dylan wanted to scream from the powerful sensations coursing through her body.

"Adam," she managed to gasp, as his hand continued its downward journey, searching out the clip on the top of her shorts. This was easily found and quickly undone as was the zipper beneath it. Adam slipped his fingers beneath the waistband of her shorts, pulling them down. Dylan helped by struggling out of them, as quickly as she could. When she would have done the same with her panties, Adam's voice came thickly from somewhere near her breasts, stopping only long enough to utter hoarsely, "No, let me."

He had the small scrap of lace removed in less than a heartbeat. Dylan's womanly mound was exposed to his wandering hand. He trailed his fingertips over her hips before moving downwards to her thighs where he tantalised her senses, slowly teasing his fingers over the insides of her legs, just out of reach of their ultimate destination. Dylan was filled with a delicious ache as his mouth followed the trail his fingertips had made, scorching Dylan's skin with their tantalising touch. Flames of desire leapt within her and she groaned ecstatically, arching herself upwards as her body released a tide of passion that she wasn't able to hold back. His mouth continued to savage her lovingly. "Oh, Adam," she moaned feverishly, grabbing at him as her body shook uncontrollably still in the throes of a mind blowing climax. *What sweet joy*, her mind sang as her body gradually started to relax, before he started his delicious onslaught, yet again. Within seconds, her heightened senses were spiralling upwards once more to meet him.

Dylan couldn't even manage the simple task of undressing him. She was like a mindless fool, a puppet for him to manipulate in any way he chose. Her body was swimming in a euphoric whirlpool of sensation. Her shaking hands couldn't manage to undo the clasps that kept him from her. After what seemed like hours to Dylan, but in reality was only a matter of seconds, Adam had removed the offending garments. They joined hers on the floor, leaving Dylan to gaze at his manhood in full arousal. She wasn't sure how much longer she could hold back the waves of desire that kept threatening to wash over her. Her body throbbed yet again, needing to be one with his, nothing less would do.

"Adam, please, please take me now," she moaned, begging him for a release from the exquisite torture he was again raining down on her.

"Soon, Sweetheart, soon. I want you to have it all," Adam continued to kiss her, his tongue searching out the hidden darkness of her mouth, while his fingers fondled her, yet again, in her most secret place. Her body was drowning, screaming with the pleasurable sensations that were being lovingly lavished on it. Dylan was trembling uncontrollably; she had reached her limit and pleadingly moaned again for Adam to take her.

Masterfully, he positioned his body over hers using his legs to prise her legs apart, before sliding himself inside her silken softness and emitting a low guttural moan of complete surrender Dylan welcomed him. Their bodies moved in complete harmony as Adam forged himself repeatedly into her, until they both lay completely spent, wrapped in the circle of each other's arms. Never before had Dylan known such an explosion of raw passion. She was utterly consumed by the wonder of it.

The shrill ring of the telephone awoke them. They were still embracing, still feeling the euphoria from their love making. Dylan was reluctant to move, she wanted to remain here, cocooned within the warmth and safety of Adam's strong embrace. She slowly climbed out of bed. "This had better be important," she mumbled to herself, as she shrugged into her dressing gown before leaving the room.

"Hello," she said, picking up the receiver and a smile spread across her face as she recognised the voice of her mother on the other end of the line.

Dylan glanced up at Adam who had followed her out, her eyebrows shooting skywards as she looked at him; his only article of clothing being a brief pair of underpants. Covering the mouthpiece with her hand, she told him frantically, "It's my mother!"

She felt ridiculous. She'd actually felt embarrassed, thinking her mother could see Adam standing there. She couldn't tear her eyes away from him. God, he looked good, so masculine and so sexy. Her mother's voice brought her back to the present, asking her when she thought she'd be down for the boys.

Dragging her eyes away from Adam, Dylan tried to concentrate on her mother's words, "Er . . . um . . . yes, yes, Mum, I'll be there first thing in the morning. Mum, I'll be bringing someone with me."

"Who?" questioned her mother, already curious.

"Adam Rossiter. You know, the man I told you about." There was a slight pause, then Dylan answered, "Yes, him. He came back to see us."

Dylan watched Adam raise his eyebrows as he listened to her side of the conversation. She tried to push him away playfully so he couldn't hear what her mother was saying.

Hanging up the phone a short time later, Dylan told him, "It seems my two brats have been telling mum and dad about you. They're dying to meet you. I wonder what the boys have said. The mind boggles at the thought."

"Never mind what the boys have said, I'm more interested in what their mother had to say," Adam mused, looking at her with a wicked gleam in his eyes.

"Nothing really. I told them how you'd broken down outside the house, also that I'd asked you to stay because of the storm," Dylan stated, not adding how shocked her mother had been upon hearing this piece of news, "mum then went on to tell me how dangerous it was to have let you in at all. She said we all could have been murdered in our beds. You know how mothers are. Anyway, I finally convinced her you were completely harmless. I told her there was nothing to worry about," Dylan had to fight her emotions to keep from laughing as she delivered that final statement.

"Harmless, hey!" he cautioned, as he advanced towards her.

Dylan knew from past experience that she was in for some sort of retribution, so she started to back away. She wasn't quick enough. "Adam, don't," she pleaded laughing uncontrollably as he started to tickle her around the area of her ribcage, "I hate being tickled. Please . . . stop. I take it back," she shrieked, as she dropped to the floor, trying unsuccessfully to get away from his lean fingers as they attacked her without mercy. Her attempts to get at him proved to be unfruitful with the end result being a tangle of arms and legs on the kitchen floor, accompanied by much laughter from the both of them, until they declared a truce with Adam helping her to her feet.

"It will be good to see the boys. I've got something for them too," Adam declared, patting Dylan affectionately on the behind as he gently pushed her out of the kitchen.

"Adam, you won't spoil them will you, by buying them things? It isn't necessary," Dylan implored, turning around to face him.

"No, Sweetheart, I won't, but I think it's important they know I care for them, too, as well as their mother. I hope you'll care for Terri in the same way," Adam replied, in answer to her question.

"If she's anything like her father, I won't be able to help myself," Dylan confessed, swallowing the lump forming in her throat.

"Come on," Adam said quietly, as he led the way back to the bedroom.

Chapter Four

Dylan was the first one to spot the boys. They were sitting on her parent's fence, obviously keeping a look out for her arrival. Their faces lit up with pleasure when they saw who was in the passenger seat of their mother's car.

"Mummy, Uncle Adam," they yelled together, as they raced to open Adam's door.

"You came back, Uncle Adam. We told mummy you would," Danny stated, then Glen added, "Mummy cried and said you wouldn't be back, but we knew you'd come for us. You promised."

"Boys, be quiet," begged Dylan of her sons.

"Mommy cried, huh?" Adam mused, putting an arm around her shoulder, pulling her close to his side.

"Don't go getting big headed," Dylan advised him, totally embarrassed, hoping her sons wouldn't see fit to inform him about too many other things she'd done over the past couple of weeks. She didn't want him to see her as a love sick fool.

"I wouldn't dream of it," Adam responded. His eyes held a hint of mischief as he gazed down at her.

"Good. Come on in and meet mum and dad," she offered, taking his hand in hers. Natalie had already toddled inside. She could now be heard talking baby talk to her doting grandparents.

Dylan's parents were sitting at the kitchen table. Morning tea had been prepared in readiness for their arrival. Dylan felt like she was going before the grand jury. She wanted her parents to like Adam. She wanted them to see his strength, his integrity, the person she'd fallen in love with.

"Hello, Mum, Dad," Dylan felt suddenly nervous. She felt Adam squeeze her hand reassuringly, letting her know everything was going to be alright.

Adam was completely natural as he spoke to Dylan's parents, answering their questions with a casual ease. He had the knack of putting people at their ease so it wasn't very long before everyone was involved in conversation. He caught Dylan looking at him and winked at her as he continued talking to her father about his work.

He was saying, "As long as you don't start believing the stuff the papers write about you. If I'd only done half the things I was said to have done, I'd need to be Superman. It's not all glitz and glamour as most people seem to think, its working long hours and if you're on location, you can be away for months at a time. Depending on where you are, it can be good or bad. My last film was shot in Africa. It was hot, we were eaten alive by mosquitoes, bogged in mud, you know, all the fun things. Filming was held up by the rain, so that put us behind for a while."

They talked for a while longer about Adam's work. Dylan realised how sick he must get of all the publicity and all of the endless questions he was expected to answer and why he treasured his private life, guarding it so astutely. How easy it would be to be misquoted. Dylan hoped their relationship could be kept secret from the press. She suddenly realised how dramatically her life would be changing. She had nothing to compare it with. The idea scared her silly. What if she failed Adam once they were in America? It would be too late to back out. Life certainly wouldn't be like it was now. She'd never thought of it before, but her lifestyle must seem very mundane to him and she wondered yet again what it was that attracted him to her. Her home was probably very different to the lavish properties he owned as well. She loved her little house, but for the first time she wondered did it seem plain to Adam. Did he think it lacked all of the luxuries he took for granted. There was so much she had to ask him. Looking around the table, Dylan realised everyone was staring at her. She'd been so deep in thought, she'd lost track of the conversation.

"What?" she asked frowning at the people who were looking at her so intently. "I'm sorry, I wasn't listening."

"We were wondering if you wanted to stay for the day. Adam said he'd like to. How about you?" her mother asked her again. Dylan realised just how much of the general conversation she'd missed. She'd been so deep in her own thoughts; she hadn't heard a single word of the conversation that had been taking place around her.

"Yes, I'd like that," Dylan told them simply, looking across at Adam for confirmation. He was looking at her shrewdly; his chin resting on his hands as he contemplated her across the table. His eyes had a puzzled look, but they told her now was not the time to find out what it was that bothered her. Dylan smiled at him, telling him silently with her large expressive eyes that everything was fine. His answering smile was all the encouragement she needed right now. Why did she have doubts anyway? This should be a happy time for her and she wasn't going to spoil their time together by brooding over situations she had no control over. Dylan changed the subject by asking how her children had behaved.

"Good as usual, with a few exceptions," answered her mother.

"What exceptions?" Dylan wanted to know, glancing at her sons. She knew they weren't about to tell her.

"Nothing you and your brothers didn't get up to when you were their age," put in her father.

"That bad!" Dylan said ironically, giving her boys the evil eye.

"Adam, would you fancy something a bit stronger than tea to drink?" Dylan's father asked, "Tea's alright for the ladies. Come with me. I'll show you what I'm trying to do in the shed."

"Watch out for dad's brew, Adam, it's lethal," Dylan joked, as Adam followed her father from the room. There was a fridge in the shed where her father kept his home brew. This was where her brothers and father would disappear to, when they were all together. It was a good sign. It meant Adam had been accepted by her father, who was usually a good judge of character.

Alone with her mother, Dylan asked, "What do you think of him, Mum?"

"I like him. He seems to be very down to earth for a film star," her mother told her honestly, "but more to the point, what do you think of him?"

"I love him," Dylan stated smiling at the old fashioned term her mother had used to describe Adam's profession. It would be hopeless trying to hide the truth from her mother.

"I thought so. It shows. Does Adam feel the same way about you?" her mother questioned.

"He says he does, but Mum it's all happening so fast. What if I'm making another mistake? I couldn't bear to be hurt again."

"Just follow your heart, Dylan, it will tell you which way you should go. I fell in love with your father the first time I saw him and he with me. We've had a good marriage based on love, trust, respect and most of all, friendship. Your father is my best friend. Our love has never wavered in all these years. Hopefully, that's how it will be for you and Adam. You're the only one who can answer those questions."

"It will mean going to live in America. I'll miss you all," Dylan confessed, as her eyes filled with unshed tears at the thought of leaving behind all that was familiar to her.

"Don't upset yourself, Love. I'm sure you'll be back to see us. Maybe I can talk your father into coming to see you," Dylan's mother told her reassuringly, then tacked on as an afterthought, "The world's not so big anymore, not with all those fast planes they have to get you from place to place."

"I suppose so. I wonder what dad and Adam are talking about?" Dylan asked her mother.

"Probably the same thing we are if I know your father. The boys seem to like him if the way they talk about him is any indication."

"You don't think dad's giving Adam the third degree, do you?" Dylan stated, getting to her feet. The last thing she wanted was for Adam to feel pressured into talking about their relationship.

"I wouldn't say the third degree exactly. More of an interrogation probably," Dylan's mother told her blandly.

"Mum! That's not funny!" Dylan said, trying to sound indignant, but failed miserably, "I'd better go and rescue him, I suppose."

Her mother's cheerful chuckle followed her outside, as she walked across the yard, towards her father's shed. There were so many memories here from her childhood. Things she'd wanted to share with her own children about the place where she'd grown up.

"Hi, you two," Dylan announced her presence as she walked into her father's sanctuary. Her father and Adam were sitting at one of the benches her father used to construct his many masterpieces. Her mother had his works of art all over the house, regardless of what she thought of them. They'd been lovingly made, so that made them priceless to her.

Dylan had to admit Adam looked at home amongst her father's things. They were drinking stubbies straight from the bottle, her father didn't believe in dressing things up. Adam was being shown how to take apart an outboard motor in minute detail. Dylan thought he must be bored to death.

"What did I tell you, Adam," retorted Dylan's father smugly, "I told you it would only be a matter of time before the women came out to get us," To Dylan he said, "You picked a winner this time, Love. I like him. We've had a good talk. I'm sure you'll be very happy."

Dylan looked apprehensively at them both, "Dad, what have you been saying? I hope you didn't embarrass Adam by asking him anything stupid did you?" Dylan could imagine her father coming straight to the point and asking Adam what his intentions were towards his daughter. She knew from past experience just how direct her father could be. Growing up, she'd lost the odd boyfriend because of her father's outspokenness and absolute directness.

Her mother had followed her out, going to stand next to her husband. Looking at them, Dylan realised what it was her mother had said to her about togetherness. They were still a striking couple;

they'd grown old gracefully and still had a lot of years to look forward to.

Before her father could answer, Adam said, "No, actually we had a good talk. I now know some things about you I didn't know before." Adam chuckled, winking at her suggestively.

"Dad, what've you been saying?" She didn't get the chance to find out and she wasn't sure she wanted to know anyway.

Danny and Glen came bursting into the shed, both of them crying and yelling at each other. "Mummy, Danny hit me," sobbed Glen, flinging himself at his mother for protection.

"He hit me first because I wouldn't give him my car to play with," Danny wailed in defence of his actions towards his brother.

"Alright both of you settle down, now!" declared Dylan firmly, "Danny, apologise to Glen for hitting him. Glen, you have plenty of cars of your own without taking any of your brother's."

The two boys glared mutinously at each other, neither of them willing to give in. Danny's blue eyes, so like her own, stared at her defiantly, while Glen's little mouth trembled slightly as he tried not to cry. Dylan's heart went out to him, but she knew she had to be firm. If she gave in to them, she knew she'd be the one to suffer in the long run. She was reminded of a Mexican standoff and had to stifle a smile behind her hand, "Well. I'm waiting," she demanded in her sternest voice.

Danny looked as if he was prepared to argue his case, but thought better of it after glancing at his mother's face. He knew from past experience that it was a hopeless cause. He decided to give in gracefully.

"I suppose you can have it!" but he was determined to have the last word as he said smugly to his brother, "It's broken anyway."

"Does this happen often?" Adam wanted to know. He'd been trying to repress a smile the whole time and now gave in to the impulse. He couldn't help it; he'd seen the funny side of the situation from an onlooker's point of view.

"I don't think it's funny and neither will you when you're living in the midst of it. Are you sure you don't want to change your mind?" Dylan frowned at him. He was standing there so calmly, obviously enjoying her displeasure.

"No, I don't want to change my mind. Danny, Glen come with me," Adam called to the two boys. The note of authority in his voice had them scurrying after him, without a word.

"Dad, what makes you so sure Adam and I are right for each other? The thought of going to America terrifies me. America is so far away from here. What if our relationship falls apart?" Dylan told her father when Adam was out of earshot. She was reminded of other times in the past sitting in this very same shed, when she'd come to her father for advice, when she'd needed answers to problems that bothered her.

"Do you love him, Dylan? Can you look into your heart and tell me you could let him walk away without a part of you going with him?" The questions were simple. Dylan knew the answers already.

"Yes, Dad, I love him, more than I thought it was possible to love anyone," Dylan announced calmly, her face softening as she thought of the man she loved.

"There's your answer then, Love," stated her father noticing the glow on his daughter's face, also, the tender note that had come into her voice as she spoke about Adam.

Turning around to walk back into the house, Dylan was surprised to see Adam standing in the doorway and was pulled up short at the sight of him. He'd obviously been listening to the conversation she'd just had with her father. Dylan's father kept on walking. After all, it hadn't been so long that he'd forgotten the madness of being caught in those first heady throes of love. He plucked a red rose from the garden, before he walked into the house with a token of love for his own special lady.

Alone with Adam, Dylan felt embarrassed, she didn't know what to say, "Hasn't anyone ever told you it's impolite to eavesdrop?"

"Did you mean that?" Adam wanted to know. His voice was soft, having almost a breathless quality to it.

Dylan tried to say yes, but couldn't seem to get the word past the lump that had formed in her throat. She had to content herself with nodding her head. She felt like crying and didn't know why. She knew her eyes were suspiciously bright with unshed tears.

Adam stood directly in front of her now, he was very close, but didn't attempt to touch her. Dylan found she couldn't look at him directly, so contented herself with focusing her gaze on the top button of his shirt, noting not for the first time, the way the hair on his chest curled tightly. How she loved to touch it, to run her fingers through its silky softness, but at the moment she was acting like a stranger, afraid to look at him lest she'd see derision for herself lurking in his green eyes. Adam finally broke the silence between them. He lifted her chin up with his little finger so that she was forced to look at him as he asked, "Why won't you look at me, Dylan?"

"I don't know what I'll see there," Dylan whispered.

"Would you like me to tell you?" and not waiting for an answer he continued, "You'll see a man who's head over heels in love with you," He kissed her lightly on the lips, before adding, "You'll see a man who wants to protect you from all of the hurts you've suffered," He kissed her again, more intently this time and then whispered against her lips, "And last, but not least, you'll see a man who desperately wants to marry you, to spend the rest of his life making you happy." The kiss that he gave her was rich and deep, robbing her mouth of all of its sweetness, but Dylan gave herself freely, returning his kiss forgetting everything except her need for this man.

"How many times do I have to tell you I love you?" Adam whispered thickly into her ear. He held her close. Dylan savoured the feel of him; she felt his body grow taut as he reacted to her nearness. She wanted to nourish the bond that was growing between them. She moved even closer to him, feeling restricted by their respective clothing.

"Always," she sighed, bringing his lips back to her own, shamelessly wanting more of him, all of him.

Blissfully lost in each other, momentarily unaware of their surroundings they found delight in one another, savouring the closeness between them. They were brought back to earth by the sound of giggling from the doorway. Striving to catch their breath, they turned around to see Danny and Glen staring at them.

"Okay, you two, what's so funny?" Adam smiled down at the two small figures standing next to them.

"You and mummy, yuk! Do grownups do that all the time?" Glen wanted to know. His mother and Uncle Adam certainly did. They always seemed to be kissing. He could think of much better things to do, like playing with his toys or riding his bike.

"Of course not, mummy and daddy never used to kiss. Daddy used to yell at mummy, don't you remember, Glen? Mummy used to cry," Danny answered Glen's question, being the eldest he thought he knew all the answers.

Looking at her sons, Dylan realised just how much they'd been through in their young lives. She knelt down beside them, putting an arm around each of them, pulling them close to her. "Boys, I don't know how to explain, but sometimes mummy's and daddy's stop loving each other. Daddy and I . . . well, we, we . . . that happened to us. We both still love you very much though. Don't ever forget that, will you?"

"Will daddy ever come home?" Danny wanted to know.

"No, Sweetheart, he won't," Dylan held her two sons to herself, hoping they'd understood. She also hoped they'd accept Adam in the role as their stepfather.

"Is Uncle Adam going to be our new daddy?" Danny asked. It seemed he'd appointed himself spokesman for the two of them.

Dylan looked up at Adam, not sure how to answer that particular question. Adam knelt down to join the threesome on the ground. "Do you want me to be your stepfather?" he asked, coming straight to the point.

"Will that mean you and mummy will fight and mummy will cry again?" Danny asked, from the protection of his mother's arms.

"No, Danny, it means that you, Glen and Natalie and your mother will come to live with me in America and we'll be happy together. I'd like to be your dad, but only if that's what you want," Adam told the two small boys, as they looked up at him, "Of course that doesn't mean you have to forget your real dad, you know," he added, as an afterthought.

It only took a moment before two small voices chorused, "Yes, please, we like you."

Adam enveloped the trio standing before him into his arms saying, "I like you a lot, too. I love your mom very much and I promise I won't make her cry . . . ever."

"Mummy's crying now, look," Glen pointed to his mother's face. Tears were rolling freely down her cheeks.

Dylan wiped the tears from her eyes, before telling them, "These are happy tears. I'm crying because I'm happy. Go and tell Nana we'll be in soon."

Danny and Glen headed for the house to do their mother's bidding, but stopped after a few steps and started to whisper excitedly to each other. By mutual consent they turned and came back to stand in front of Dylan and Adam looking at them where they were still crouched on the ground.

"Yes," Dylan said, wanting to know the reason for her sons' return.

"Well, we were just wondering if we can go to Disneyland when we get to . . . to . . . Am . . . where is it we're going again, Mummy?" Danny asked his mother with Glen looking on expectantly. Both boys had huge smiles plastered on their faces.

"I don't know. Perhaps you'd better ask Adam that question," Dylan told them looking at Adam to gauge his response to her children's inquiry.

Two pair of eyes looked at Adam. Dylan could see the hope shinning out of their eyes as they waited for his answer.

"I think that could be arranged," Adam smilingly told Danny and Glen and within seconds they were jumping around with the sheer joy of knowing that they would be going to Disneyland.

Pushing himself up from the ground, Adam held out his hand to Dylan and would have pulled her to her feet, but she motioned for him to sit back down. She didn't give him a chance to say a word. She straddled him to sit on his lap with her legs linked behind his back. She started kissing him with abandon, telling him softly between kisses how much she loved him. Her caresses were getting bolder as her ardour grew. At first, she didn't notice he wasn't responding as she would have liked. She wanted to give him pleasure at this moment and that thought alone was making her senses soar.

"Dylan," Adam whispered hoarsely, trying unsuccessfully to push her away.

"Mmm," she continued, nuzzling his ear with her lips.

"Dylan," he insisted, as she ground her body wantonly against his.

Dylan heard his voice coming to her through an emotional fog. Her hand had started to wander down towards his groin, but to her surprise his hand snaked out to stop her.

"Dylan," he croaked again, "please!"

"Adam, what is it?" she questioned, looking up at him through passion glazed eyes.

He looked uncomfortably at her for a few seconds, before he looked past her over her shoulder, towards the door of the shed. It took her a minute or so to realise they weren't alone. "Oh, no!" she muttered, burying her head into the neck she'd only seconds before been kissing, "Please tell me there's no one there?"

Adam gave her a silly look that confirmed her worst fears. Turning around, she said the first thing that came into her head, "Hello, Mum, Dad. I didn't see you there."

"Obviously. We came out to tell you lunch is nearly ready," her mother told them. Despite what she'd just witnessed, she felt very happy for her daughter. She'd been worrying about her. She needed someone in her life, besides her children; someone who would take care of her and love her.

Dylan's face had turned a bright red. She defended herself by saying, "I can't help it, I love him."

"Glad to hear it," Dylan's father said matter-of-factly. To his wife, he said, "Emily, I think we'd better feed these two before Dylan goes completely overboard."

Adam helped Dylan to her feet and this time she didn't oppose him. "Why didn't you tell me!" she exclaimed, giving him a thump on his arm. She couldn't remember ever feeling so embarrassed in front of her parents, but then, she'd never been found in such a compromising position before either.

Adam looked at her in mock horror, throwing his arms up into the air before he, too, started to walk away towards the house leaving her standing there staring after them all. He was muttering to himself about silly women, before the three of them started to laugh. Dylan wanted to follow them, but found she couldn't, she really felt foolish.

Suddenly, Adam pivoted on his heel and made his way back to where Dylan stood and grabbing her arm, he led her towards the house. He whispered in her ear, "We'll finish what you started as soon as we get home, Sexpot, as . . . soon . . . as . . . we . . . get . . . home." He emphasised the last few words slowly and clearly, gazing directly into her eyes as he did so. "Understood!"

"Yes, Adam," Dylan answered so meekly, Adam looked down at her in genuine surprise, wondering what was wrong.

"Honey, they understand. I wouldn't mind betting they've been sprung once or twice either," He kissed her gently on the lips, before guiding her inside to their waiting family.

Adam had to leave early the next day, but not before promising to phone her that night. Dylan took her children over to see their horses, feeling pleased they had the same love of the land that she possessed. As always, Dylan could feel the peace of the countryside settle around her like a protective cloak. She watched her boys ride their horses around the small paddock located close to the house. They were both good riders even at this early age. *Jake had taught them, at least they'd agreed on something,* thought Dylan, refusing to let the thought of Jake make her unhappy.

Dylan's mare was standing patiently waiting. She was a Palomino Dylan had owned for many years, even before she'd met Jake. She was fifteen hands high and was now twelve years old.

Taking sugar cubes from her pocket, Dylan laughed, when she heard Sascha nicker for them.

"Come on, you spoilt thing, earn your oats," Dylan said to her beloved horse as she sprang up onto her back. She rode over to where Rae and Tom were casually leaning against the fence rails, watching Danny and Glen ride around the small enclosure.

"I won't be long. Can you spare me a few minutes when I get back, Rae?" Dylan wanted to tell Rae about Adam. How she'd managed to keep their relationship to herself for this long was beyond her as it was.

"Sure, go ahead," Rae smiled, glancing at her friend thinking she looked different somehow.

Dylan waved as she turned the mare's head and giving her a gentle kick, urged her into a canter that would take them away from the house towards the creek and the distant trees. It wasn't long before Dylan reached her destination, a shady spot by the creek sheltered by the trees, a perfect spot in Dylan's estimation. In times gone by, Dylan would come here to think, especially when she and Jake had quarrelled. Dylan felt at peace here, letting the tranquillity of her surroundings wash over her. She took the bridle from her horse's head, knowing she'd come when she was called.

Was it her imagination, or did everything seem different? Dylan hadn't been here since meeting Adam, so she reasoned that it was she who'd changed, not the place. Before, she used to come here to cry, to lick her wounds before going back to an intolerable situation, then, because she'd been alone for so long, this place became a refuge where she'd come to think about the happenings going on in her life, like now. Dylan was struck by the beauty of her surroundings. There was new growth after the recent storms, everything was green and lush.

From her position sitting here against a tree, Dylan had a good view of the paddocks and in the distance she could clearly see her friend's house. Some of the cows that formed part of Tom's dairy herd grazed nearby. The creek ran gently at this time of year, the recent rain hadn't made much difference to its depth as it gurgled peacefully over the rocks. The paper barks and gum trees completed an already perfect picture. Dylan could hear kookaburras laughing in the nearby trees, and looking up she saw two of them sitting side by side. She wondered if they were mates. In the past, she'd also spied the occasional koala curled up fast asleep in the branches of the gum trees.

"I'll miss this place . . . and Rae and Tom," Dylan spoke to the beauty around her. She had to smile as she thought of her friends. At least they were happy, disgustingly so, laughed Dylan to herself, thinking of one particular time when Tom had met them for lunch. They hadn't cared one whit about who had seen them demonstrate their love for each other. Dylan could remember feeling embarrassed, but still sincerely happy for them, never having felt so deeply for anyone. *Until now,* she thought.

Thinking of Adam gave her a warm glow in the region of her heart, as she remembered the night before. They'd arrived home, put the sleeping children to bed and then Adam had led the way to the bedroom. He'd shut the door behind them.

"That's so you can't get away. I didn't think I'd last the distance. I've had images of you on my mind all day, Witch," He'd held out his arms in an open invitation. Dylan had happily stepped into them, into paradise.

Their love making surpassed any that had gone before. Their senses seemed heightened; they were tuned into each other's needs and wants. Dylan actually cried out with pleasure, so intense was her memory of the night before. Coming back to the present was painful, because Adam wasn't there with her. Afterwards, he'd held her gently within the circle of his arms; they'd both been trembling, so great was the emotion they'd experienced.

Later, as they'd sat eating a late night snack, Adam had told her about a farm he knew of back home that was for sale, "It belongs to a friend. I wasn't interested before, but now . . . ," he'd paused, looking at Dylan, wanting confirmation, "It will give us the privacy we want to live any sort of a normal life, or would you prefer to live in the house I'm in now?"

"I don't know. Can you get any photos of the place? I'll leave it up to you." Dylan had told him, not knowing how to handle all of the changes she'd have to go through in the coming months, not to mention the rest of her life. Although, the thought of living on the land held an immense appeal and it would keep her and her children away from inquisitive, prying eyes. These changes in her life were happening way too fast. She hoped she'd be able to cope, and would be able to deal with being a part of Adam's life. His life style was so vastly different from her own. She remembered hesitating before she'd asked him, "Adam, are there any loose ends that need cutting off before I arrive?" She didn't want to be confronted by any jealous rivals.

"I'll have you know I've lived the life of a monk!" Adam had exclaimed fervently, giving Dylan a mortified look, while crossing his heart with his hand.

"I'll bet you have, Adam Rossiter. I'll just bet you have." Her thoughts were interrupted by Sascha, who had wandered over to where Dylan was sitting. She was trying to get at the sugar cubes she knew Dylan kept in her pocket. Dylan regretfully pushed her thoughts of Adam to the back of her mind, knowing it was time to start back.

Walking towards the house, Dylan could hear her children talking to Rae and Tom, *no doubt about Adam,* she thought, as she came closer and was able to hear their excited chatter. *Oh, well, I was going to tell them anyway, wasn't I?* Dylan knew her friends would be pleased for her, but darn it, she'd wanted to tell them. *I sound like one of my children throwing a hissy fit,* Dylan thought and smiled at her childish antics.

Glancing around her at the farm buildings and the land beyond, Dylan knew she'd miss this place almost as much as her own home. Rae and Tom were fully self-sufficient, growing everything they needed themselves. They had a small dairy herd that provided them with their primary income and Tom was also branching out into breeding horses. He'd been working with a very promising colt when they'd arrived earlier. Tom believed in efficiency and as always, everything was spic and span and in good running order. Dylan had walked through the barn, letting the different smells on the property fill her nostrils.

"Am I too late for a cup of tea?" Dylan asked brightly, giving her sons the evil eye as she mounted the steps to sit down on one of the chairs on the verandah.

"No, not at all. I've made a fresh pot," Rae answered sweetly, "it's time we had that little chat. What is it you haven't told me, Dylan?"

Only Rae could make it sound like she wanted to discuss something as mundane as the weather. Dylan was grateful to her for that. They'd known each other long enough to dispense with any beating around the bush. Dylan searched her friend's face, seeing the concern lurking behind the light banter. Dylan had often wished she could find someone like Rae's Tom. They'd often joked about it with Dylan saying when Rae finished with him, he was to come and live with her. Rae and Tom had what Dylan thought of as a perfect marriage. Looking at her friend, Dylan realised just how badly she needed to talk to someone about Adam, to get another woman's point of view, someone other than her mother, who had been only too happy to pass on her wisdom and knowledge, to be sure, but Dylan needed to talk to her friend. Who better than Rae, Dylan trusted her completely. After all, it wouldn't be the first time they'd discussed their problems regarding members of the opposite sex.

Feeling Dylan was reluctant to talk in front of Tom, Rae fabricated an excuse, "Tom, my sweet, I think I can hear old Bob calling you to go and help him with the milking."

"Bob's not calling . . . oh, I guess he is. I'll go and see if he needs a hand," Tom sighed, as he looked at his wife who was smiling at him sweetly while helping him to his feet, before giving him an exaggerated push off the verandah.

"Honestly, men are so thick sometimes, aren't they?" she told Dylan, coming back to sit beside her on the steps, "Now, tell Aunty Rae all about it."

Dylan couldn't help but laugh at her friend's antics. Dylan suspected Rae was trying to make things easy for her by creating a relaxed atmosphere. The trouble was she didn't know where to start. She looked out over the paddocks, towards the grove of trees she'd just visited. They shimmered in the afternoon heat, giving an illusion of unreality. Dylan felt like that, like there was an illusion of unreality surrounding her. She felt like Cinderella, but she was afraid her story wouldn't have a happy ending. She wrung her hands together in an unconscious gesture as she tried to find a way to relate her story to her friend.

"Dylan?" Rae's quiet voice brought her back to the present, "Dylan, tell me what's happening?"

Haltingly at first, Dylan told Rae about Adam, about her fears, about her all-consuming love for a virtual stranger. She found it hard to believe she'd only known him for a bit over two weeks; it seemed more like a lifetime. "I feel so alive when I'm with him, Rae, so sure we can make our relationship work, so sure he really does love me, but when he has to leave and I'm alone, I wonder what he sees in me. He's surrounded by beautiful women all the time. I can't compete with them and then there's the children. I can't convince myself that he really loves me. He's a good actor, what if it's just a game to him, you know, someone to amuse himself with while he's in Australia. I love him so much. I'm in way over my head. I guess you think I'm a complete fool to have let things get so out of hand, don't you?" When her friend remained silent, Dylan looked at her, surprised to see tears falling freely down her cheeks.

Finding her voice at last, Rae declared, "I'm so happy for you. I've been worrying about you. I honestly don't know what advice to give you, never having met him, but I can assure you I plan to remedy that slight injustice on your part. Follow your heart like I did with Tom. Remember how I used to follow him around like a lost puppy when we first met. I'm not suggesting you do that with Adam though because it sounds like he might have a few too many females doing that already. Look, I don't know how Adam feels about you yet, but I can see the difference he's made to you. He's just a man after all," Rae laughed, seeing the face Dylan pulled upon hearing this last bit of information, "So treat him that way, like any other man, I mean. If it turns out badly and don't ask me why, but I have a good feeling about all of this, but just in case it doesn't, you have Tom and I to turn to . . . plus your folks. I realise we're not good substitutes under the circumstances, but we're the best I can offer," Rae finished, holding her hands in the air to demonstrate her point.

"Poor substitute, yes, definitely," Dylan joked, "but I do appreciate your offer. I'll try to remember it."

"Good. Now back to more serious matters. When am I going to meet him? I take it he'll be back next week-end? We could all have dinner, what do you say?" Rae fired the questions at her, not really expecting an answer to any of them.

"You wouldn't do anything stupid would you, Rae?" Dylan said apprehensively, knowing how straight forward her friend could be, having seen her in action with Jake. Rae was only slightly built, only coming to Dylan's shoulder. Her brown eyes could melt butter, but once angered, she could be a formidable opponent; one who made it clear she was a force to be reckoned with if the need arose.

"Why whatever do you mean?" Rae asked innocently.

"Would you like a list? When you want to find something out, you're about as subtle as a train," Dylan told her friend frankly.

"I'll be on my best behaviour, I promise not to gush once," Rae parried and then said mischievously, "Well, maybe once or twice or thrice . . ."

"Oh, god, the poor man will probably think he's gotten mixed up with a bunch of groupies," Dylan laughed uncertainly. Rae was just mad enough to do it.

"From what you've told me I reckon he might be thinking that already," Rae mused, a gleeful grin had spread over her face as she spoke.

"Rae, you're impossible. Anyway I . . . oh, never mind, I'm not going to tell you everything," Dylan finished. She couldn't help but laugh at her friend's antics. Coming to the farm today and talking to Rae was the best thing she could have done. It was better than any tonic she could have taken. She continued, "I suppose I'd better take my offspring home for tea."

"Do you want to have tea here?" Rae inquired.

"No, I'm looking forward to an early night, actually. I'm tired. I'll stay one night after work when I get the kids, okay. I'd like to talk some more. I feel really screwed up."

"See that you do," Rae said seriously and then added sounding more like her old self, "I'd hate to think I was missing out on anything. Hey, I just thought, this means I'll be out of a job. You won't need me to look after the kids anymore." This last bit was uttered sadly.

Dylan smiled solemnly at her friend, knowing how much she'd miss her charges. Looking after Dylan's children had been an act of love on Rae's part. She thought the world of all three of them. Rae and Tom were godparents to all three of Dylan's children and if anything was to ever happen to Dylan she knew they'd have a loving home to go to and a loving couple to look after them.

Chapter Five

Dylan's mood over the next few days settled into one of depression. She attributed it to the fact that when Adam had rung a few days earlier, he hadn't been able to talk longer than a few minutes. He'd told her they were working every available minute trying to catch up on their shooting schedule which was way behind because of some faulty equipment that hadn't been able to be replaced. He'd quickly asked about the children, then he'd had to go, leaving Dylan feeling hurt and confused, wondering where the man she'd fallen in love with had disappeared to.

The trouble is, she thought, *I don't know anything about him other than when he's with me. In his work, he could be quite ruthless and demanding of the people around him; a real tyrant, in fact.*

The school holidays were nearly over. Danny and Glen were bored with their own company. They needed a diversion to occupy their agile little minds. They came up with the idea of going to the beach, asking their mother in voices that were intended to win her over and give in to their way of thinking.

Dylan couldn't help but give in to the two little boys who were looking up at her so expectantly with undisguised hope shining out of their rounded eyes. Natalie added her own brand of persuasion to the argument by going to the cupboard and dragging out the beach towels.

"It looks like I'm outvoted," Dylan declared, looking down into the faces of her three children, "Alright, it's an offer too good to refuse. How about I make us up some lunch? We can eat there as well."

"Yippee!" yelled two small voices together.

"You go and put your swimmers on, then put our towels in the beach bag." *That will keep them busy for at least five minutes,* thought Dylan as she started to prepare sandwiches, making sure she put in some crusts for the sea gulls. She knew from past experience her children would feed the greedy birds their own lunch, going without themselves if she didn't provide for them, as well. Feeding the sea gulls had become a ritual, one they always performed religiously on every visit to the beach.

It was a perfect day. The sky was a beautiful azure blue with only an occasional wisp of white in sight. Dylan lived about four blocks from the beach and sometimes they walked the short distance, but today, she felt too lazy, telling herself she'd walk along the beach later on. The tiny harbour was nearly deserted when they arrived. It was mainly used by the local fishermen, who moored their fishing boats in the small inlet. When the tide was out, it wasn't unusual to see the vessels stuck fast in the sand, unable to move until the tide came back in to refloat them. Today, the tide had already started to turn which meant the boys would be able to fossick for shells and soldier crabs, both of which were in plentiful abundance on the rock strewn beach. Also, the odd sand crab could be found, some no more than an inch across.

Dylan had hardly stopped the car when Danny and Glen were clamouring to be out of its confining space. "Hey, you two take it easy!" she cautioned. The last thing she needed was an accident.

Natalie added her own small voice to those of her brothers. Soon, everyone was happily engaged building sand castles. The boys had actually conceded to let their sister join them in this mammoth task. *Poor little pet,* thought Dylan, *they really do make it hard for her sometimes. All she ever wants is to share their fun. Maybe as they grow older, they'll become more protective of her.*

Dylan was able to relax. She sat on the concrete retaining wall that formed part of the man-made barrier against the sea and the rougher elements that sometimes descended on their small community from the open sea. When the tide was fully in, it would lap against the very area where Dylan was sitting. They weren't on any tourist map, the bay hadn't gone ahead in all the years that Dylan and her family had lived here. She loved the rustic atmosphere that clung to the area with a fierce tenacity. The locals didn't seem to want change and neither did Dylan. It was off the beaten track, but all a person had to do was get in a car and drive for about fifteen minutes and they would be in the middle of Redcliffe, the city that supplied the residents with all of their needs should they feel the need to venture out of their own back yard. Not many did. They were mostly elderly people, many of whom had grown up here and probably intended to die here. Dylan had marvelled at the width of the streets in the older part of the community. They were so very narrow, a fact which was explained to her in a way that had made her laugh at the time. The streets only needed to be wide enough for a horse and cart to pass on, she'd been told. Before sewerage was introduced into the area, that's how it was done. In fact, many of the old timers still preferred to use the outhouse, but they were very few now. Dylan loved to hear the old stories that were told about the area. None of them were in any way historically important, but still, Dylan was fascinated. She'd even contemplated writing it all down one day, in the hopes of starting a book. It wouldn't hurt to have the area's history saved for posterity. But she guessed now that would never happen.

Dylan had brought a book with her, thinking that she'd be able to catch up on some reading; this was something that she liked to do, but of late, she hadn't so much as looked between the covers of a book. It seemed that today wasn't to be any different. She couldn't seem to concentrate on the plot. The words kept turning into images of Adam, his smiling face, those incredibly green eyes gazed up at her mockingly, until in exasperation, she put the book away, not having a clue what the pages had held. She decided her best course of action would be to join the trio on the beach in front of her.

The sand castle they were building had turned into a sprawling conglomeration of towers and spires which seemed to be joined by an intricate network of lane ways and bridges. Around the perimeter of this architectural masterpiece, they'd built a moat which they were trying to fill with water. To their consternation, all of their diligent efforts were for nothing, because as soon as the water was poured into the sandy causeway, it would instantly sink into the sand. Their disappointment at not being able to make the moat hold water soon turned into frustration and in a moment of anger Danny and Glen flung themselves down onto their magnificent creation, pummelling it with their feet and hands, until it once more resembled a nondescript sandy patch of beach.

"Okay," Dylan said, seeing that things could very easily get out of hand, "Who's for something to eat. I'm starving. But first, I think you two had better wash off some of that sand. You'll end up eating it."

After eating, they walked along the shoreline looking for shells to take home. Danny and Glen were kicking at the water with their feet, making a game of it, seeing who could make the biggest splash. Dylan knew it would only be a matter of time before they were saturated, but she didn't have the heart to stop them. Anyway, she berated herself that's what we're here for isn't it, to have fun, to get wet, to swim, to relax and be happy? Dylan knew these reasons were true for her children, she could see they were having a good time, having a ball in fact, judging by the noise. As for herself, well, three out of four wasn't bad, was it?

Why not admit it, a small voice inside her asked, you're missing Adam and still not terribly sure of him. Drat the man! Would she always be hounded by this sweet ecstasy whenever she thought of him, which was most of the time? Is this how a healthy relationship should be progressing? She couldn't remember being enveloped in this eternal fog of emotion when she'd been married to Jake.

Thoughts of Adam infiltrated into her mind at any given moment, to the exclusion of everything else.

Her children's happy squeals brought Dylan's thoughts back to the present. Looking around to see what was causing their hysteria, she saw Adam making his way leisurely towards them. Dylan blinked to make sure the man before her wasn't an illusion. Seeing him did strange things to her heart, its rapid beat sounded loud in her ears, almost like the sound of huge waves crashing against the shore. She had to take deep breaths of air into her lungs to steady herself. Dylan watched him, as he moved towards them, his long stride covering the distance between them in a matter of minutes. She could see his muscles rippling under the shirt he wore. It clung to his body revealing a fabulous physique. The deep tan colour suited him. His body seemed to be oozing health and vitality. It told the world he was master of all he surveyed. He wore denim cut offs which showed his thigh muscles bulging with every step he took. Large sun glasses hid his eyes, but Dylan knew he looked at her. He radiated sex appeal and just looking at him gave Dylan a lot of pleasure. He reminded her of a young lion returning to his pride, very, very sure of his ultimate victory over his intended prey. He knew submission was close at hand.

When he was about a foot away from her, he stopped and just looked down at her from behind his dark glasses. He studied her, saying nothing, a slight smile curved the corners of his mouth, before he told her softly, "God, you look good." He covered the extra foot of ground, putting his arms casually around her waist, before bringing his lips down to rest lightly on her own.

Natalie was clamouring to be picked up. She was pulling on the hem of Adam's shorts, her adoring little face turned towards him as she concentrated all of her attention on the task at hand. "Hi, Sweetheart," he said to the toddler, as he swooped her up into his arms, giving one chubby cheek a quick kiss before he settled the little girl onto his broad shoulders.

"Adam, is everything all right?" Dylan wanted to know. "I wasn't expecting you." She could smell the lingering aroma of his after-shave. It filled her nostrils and she drank it in like fine wine.

"Everything's fine. We had a break in shooting due to the rain. Rather than sit around the hotel, I decided to come up here. Cause any problems for you, Mrs Miles?"

"None I can think of at the present time, but I'll let you know if any crop up," Dylan told him chirpily, spontaneous in her reaction to him. She'd never felt this repartee with anyone else. She enjoyed their verbal efforts to outdo each other. It helped to keep her on her toes.

What Adam hadn't told her, was how he'd told the director he was taking off for parts unknown and wouldn't be available until shooting resumed. He had a clause written into his contract; one that stated he was to have a certain amount of free time to himself during filming. These were things his agent had arranged. Adam had prided himself on never calling any of these clauses into play, until now. He'd always gone along with anything the director wanted, to keep things running smoothly. Now, he was calling in some of those favours. The director had wanted to set up a series of interviews to promote the filming of the movie while they were waiting for the rain to ease. Adam had refused, but he'd had to promise to hold a press conference sometime in the near future.

"How did you know where to find us?" Dylan inquired, smiling at the way Natalie was playing with Adam's hair. Her daughter was twirling his hair around her fingers only to let it go and then start her task all over again.

She put her hand out to stop the child, thinking Adam might be getting annoyed, but he stopped her saying he didn't mind, then added in answer to Dylan's former inquiry, "I rang your cell phone, but there was no answer so I took a guess. If you weren't here, I was going to wait at home for you." He had his own key now. Dylan had given him one for reasons such as this. She wanted him to treat her home as he would his own.

"Oh, sorry. I left it in the car." Dylan told him thinking that in future she'd have to remember to take her phone with her when she got out of the car.

Danny and Glen had finished chasing soldier crabs. They were sick of stalking their prey only to have the tiny blue bugs disappear down into the sand at the last minute. Racing up to their mother and Adam, they cavorted in front of them in what they believed to be a marvellous show of athletic showmanship.

Grinning madly, Adam went down on his knees but not before swinging Natalie from her position on his shoulders to his hip, "Hi, hot shots, how've you been?" He listened intently while they related some of their adventures of the last few days to him.

They stayed another few hours at the beach until the area started to resemble a large lake that had somehow lost all of its water. The tide had receded way out and there was only a muddy residue in its place and the stench from rotting shellfish, now exposed to the sun was starting to fill their nostrils.

After a few light hearted grumbles from the boys everyone decided to call it a day, a fact which pleased Dylan greatly. She was in need of a good strong cup of coffee.

"If you guys go up to the car, there's some candy bars in the glove box. Don't eat Nat's," he called after them as they raced along the beach, eager to reach their treats. Natalie ambled along at a steadier pace; her little legs couldn't keep up with her brothers.

"Have you eaten yet?" Dylan asked him as she moved around the kitchen. They'd just arrived home. The boys were in the bath getting a much needed scrub down and Natalie had been put down for a nap. She'd been asleep as soon as her head had touched the pillow.

"Mmm, earlier on the plane," Adam was sitting on top of a kitchen bench watching her as she prepared their coffee.

Dylan handed him a steaming mug, before grabbing a stool for herself, so she could join him. He was sitting casually with one foot raised, resting on the bench, his hand supported his chin and his elbow rested on his knee. On impulse, Dylan bent down and placed a light kiss on his knee for no other reason she could think of, other than it was there. Looking up at him, she noticed he had raised his eyebrows questionably, so she told him casually, "I couldn't reach your lips."

"Oh," he answered, seeming quite content with this explanation and continued to drink his coffee.

Dylan treasured these quite moments they shared together in companionable silence. It was nice knowing she didn't have to force a conversation neither one of them felt like participating in. These times were rare, because her children demanded her attention and now Adam's also.

The silence was quickly shattered with the return to the kitchen of Danny and Glen who wanted something to eat and drink. Dylan told them she didn't know where they found the room to put all this food they were eating. She jokingly felt their tummies telling them she thought they really wanted to hide it for later on.

"No," they assured their mother solemnly, before turning to Adam asking him if he'd come down into the back yard to play cricket with them.

Watching from the window a short time later, Dylan was amused to see how the game was progressing. It had developed a few new rules and seemed to have taken on some of the characteristics of American baseball.

Dylan went through to check on Natalie, finding her sleeping peacefully, clutching her rag doll to her chest. She had adapted to sleeping in her own room straight away. In fact, she seemed to like it.

She decided she'd use this free time she'd been given to do some of the more mundane things she'd been putting off, like mending some of Danny's shirts. He was always coming home with his shirt minus a button or the hem of his shorts down. *Oh, well, boys will be boys,* she thought as she started on her task.

Taking the stairs two at a time and heading for the fridge for a much needed cold drink, Adam told the boys to do some push ups. He needed every advantage he could think off. Danny and Glen were coasting home in the game of ball they were playing. They kept changing the rules, he was sure of it. It couldn't be just luck. He walked through the house looking for Dylan. He needed some help if he was to come out of this without losing his shirt. He'd made a bet with the boys, telling them the losing team had to do the dishes after dinner tonight. So far that person appeared to be him.

"Dylan," he called as he rounded the corner leading into the lounge room, "Come and help me. They've got me licked . . . ," He stopped talking, but came further into the room. He smiled tenderly at the scene that greeted him. Dylan was sound asleep, curled up on the lounge chair. One of her hands cushioned her head, the other one, he noticed, still held the needle she'd been using to do the darning. Taking the needle from her hand, he gently picked her up then carried her to bed where he gently laid her down, careful not to wake her. She looked like one of her children, her face peaceful as she slept. He covered her with the quilt before bending down to tenderly kiss her on the lips. He whispered softly, "I could reach your lips," before turning to quietly leave the room.

Dylan awoke some time later. She'd been dreaming about Adam. He'd picked her up and carried her effortlessly to bed. He'd been kissing her, but then he stopped. Dylan put her fingers to her lips, trying to recapture the rapturous feelings from her dream. He'd left her and Dylan could remember asking, no pleading with him to stay, but still he'd left, leaving her alone. Dylan looked around the room, trying to recall how she'd gotten here. She remembered starting the mending, but had felt drowsy. She'd put her head down on the side of the lounge chair intending to rest for a few minutes. She must have walked in here in her sleep, how else could she be here, unless Adam really had carried her in to bed and then kissed her. It would explain her dream. Her subconscious mind must have registered his doing these things, causing her to dream about him. She glanced at the clock on the bedside table as she swung her legs to the floor. It was nearly four-thirty in the afternoon. Goodness, she'd slept for hours.

Dylan found everyone sitting in front of the television set, watching cartoons when she walked down the hallway a short time later. Natalie and Glen were each seated on Adam's lap, while

Danny sat beside him. Adam had an arm thrown casually around him. They made a beautiful picture of domesticity sitting there like that. It warmed Dylan's heart to see the scene before her. They were all laughing at the antics of the cartoon character and at first, didn't notice her presence. It seemed so right, so natural to see them all together like this. The bonds being formed here were as strong as any blood ties could ever be.

Turning his head, Adam saw Dylan standing there, watching them, "Hello, Sleepyhead. Did you have a good nap?" He thought she looked all ruffled, her cheeks were rosy from sleep. She presented a lovely picture standing there in the doorway, "Come and join us?" he invited softly.

Dylan joined the foursome on the couch and before long she was giggling along with them. When the show finished a short time later, Danny turned to her as if on cue, to ask, "What's to eat, Mummy, I'm hungry?"

"There's some fruit in the basket and milk in the fridge. That ought to keep you going until tea time, shouldn't it?" The look on his face told Dylan fruit and milk wasn't the sort of snack he'd had in mind.

"It's that or nothing, Sport," Dylan was adamant and wouldn't budge.

Danny looked at Adam for support, but Adam shrugged his shoulders regretfully. "Take a tip from one of the boys, Danny, quit while you're ahead," He then looked at Dylan saying, "I love a woman who's masterful." His deep chuckle rang out around the room before he brought his lips down to meet hers, silencing any protest she might have made. He continued, "How about we take the kids out for tea tonight? Do you feel up to it? You still look tired; maybe we should just have an early night."

"No! We want to go out for tea. Please, Mummy," two voices yelled in unison from the kitchen, before two heads popped around the corner to stare at her, while they waited for an answer.

"It seems I'm outvoted. Actually, it would be nice to go somewhere. I don't feel like cooking," Dylan smiled, hearing the delight in her children's voices. At times like this, she knew she missed the companionship of a man in her life, sharing the little pleasures everyday family life could bring.

The only dark cloud on Dylan's horizon was the fact that Adam would be recognised and would most likely be swamped by fans clamouring for his attention, but she kept this fear to herself.

Later that night, as they drove into the car park of the family restaurant the boys had chosen, Dylan was dismayed to see so many of the spaces had already been taken. She'd been hoping they'd have the place to themselves. She instantly felt her stomach muscles tighten, not sure now if she wanted to go through with the evening after all. If Adam was recognised, how would she handle such a situation? She took a deep breath, feeling like someone about to do battle.

Noticing this gesture, Adam put an arm around her shoulder pulling her closer to his side, "Don't worry, Honey, even if anyone does recognise me, most people leave you alone once they've established who you are. It's only the press who hound you all the time."

"I'm fine really, I'm just nervous," Dylan acknowledged, pushing her doubts to the back of her mind. She was determined to enjoy the evening, in spite of herself.

"Come on, the troops are getting restless over there," Adam urged, as he led her towards the door.

Dylan could see Danny and Glen waiting impatiently by the big swing doors, their little eyes as big as saucers, *probably figuring how much food they could eat before they were sick,* she thought. Natalie was wriggling to get down wanting to join her brothers.

Only when they'd given their order and had been shown to their corner table, a fact that Dylan secretly cheered, for she wouldn't feel so conspicuous now, was she able to relax. She glanced at Adam and found him looking at her.

"Was that so bad?" he asked, before adding, "Have I told you how beautiful you look tonight, Sweetheart?" He had one of her hands in his; his long sensuous fingers were caressing hers in a casual way that belied his true feelings. He'd wanted to put her at ease; he could feel the tenseness she was trying so hard to hide as he touched her.

"You don't look bad yourself," Dylan returned the compliment, feeling her pulses quicken as she looked at him. Her face took on a dreamy look as she thought of his body lying next to hers, his strength and vitality flowing from him to her as he loved her.

Adam's hand caressing her face across the table brought her back to the present. "Hey, where did you go to? You were miles away."

Dylan felt her cheeks burn as she gazed across at him, wishing they were home. She wanted to bring her fantasy to life.

It seemed her startled looks were enough to convey to him what manner of things she'd been thinking, because he smiled at her with a wicked gleam in his green eyes that told her, without the need for words that he understood, he felt the same way himself.

The timely arrival of their food saved Dylan from any embarrassing explanations. Danny and Glen were beside themselves with happiness at being able to choose their own meal. They were now in the process of swapping food with each other. *They were a disaster about to happen,* Dylan thought, if she didn't keep an eye on them. "If you two keep this up you'll spill food all over yourselves. Just eat what's on your own plate," Dylan told them, secretly amused by their antics.

"Let them go, Love, I'm keeping an eye on them. You watch Natalie, she's dipping chips into her drink," Adam said, taking charge of the situation.

Towards the end of their meal, just when Dylan was starting to relax, thinking they were going to have an incident free evening, the bubble burst. She was busy with Natalie, so didn't see the people at the table across from them looking at Adam, covertly at first and then with mounting excitement as they realised who he was. His accent was one of the things that gave them a clue as to his identity, that and the fact that they'd just been to see one of his movies, they informed him later.

One of their children, a boy of about ten or eleven years old came over to the alcove where they were sitting to ask Adam shyly, "Excuse me, but are you Adam Finlayson?"

Dylan felt her breath catch in her throat threatening to gag her, as she turned to see who had asked the question she'd least wanted to hear. She was starting to panic, she turned to Adam; she'd take her cue from him. He must have had to face this situation many times during his career. Dylan could see a subtle change in his manner, although it was not very perceptible to those around them, she could also see that his carefree manner of a few seconds ago had gone, it had been replaced by the professional in him, the other Adam; the one that she didn't know. He was sitting calmly, smiling at the child. It was obvious the boy was awe struck. He was actually meeting one of his heroes. Here was a story he'd tell his friends over and over again for a long time to come.

Adam answered the boy casually, "Yes, I am."

Dylan was conscious of many things happening at once. Everyone in their immediate vicinity seemed to stop eating and talking to look in their direction, wanting to confirm the story that was circulating around the restaurant.

"Wow!" the boy was awe struck; he just stared at Adam as if he was looking at a god, "I think you're great. Can I please have your autograph?" Dylan could see the child was close to tears. She knew Adam would comply with his request.

"Sure, son. Dylan, have you got a pen?" Adam asked her quietly. This started a cue; it seemed everyone wanted a piece of the action. Adam signed the endless flow of autographs without comment, but he refused to answer any questions of a personal nature, just saying he was in Australia making a movie and would be leaving for the States shortly.

After what seemed like a lifetime to Dylan, Adam told everyone he was sorry, but he had to go. She didn't know how Adam stood all the hype. She understood now why he'd remained silent about his true identity when they'd first met. To have this happen everywhere you went, to have to live with the blatant adoration of his fans, to have to live up to their standards of him couldn't be an easy task. No wonder he was so maniacal about his personal life being kept strictly personal. Dylan was sure that when they left the restaurant someone would go so far as to take the leftovers from his plate to keep as a souvenir.

On their way out, Adam had gone over to the boy's table where he sat with his parents. *He makes people feel special,* Dylan thought, as she watched him talking to the child. "Bye, Peter, you be good for your mom and dad, now," he said, before walking back over to where Dylan waited for him by the door.

"That was nice. The little fellow won't forget you, or this night in a hurry," Dylan told him, as they walked over to their car, "Does that happen often?"

"Pretty much, you get used to it after a while," he answered nonchalantly.

Danny and Glen had loved every minute of it. To them, it had been a great adventure. Dylan had been hard pressed to keep them quiet. She was sure that if they'd been given the chance, they would have told all they knew to anybody who happened to ask. That would prove to be choice reading if it reached the media. She realised she'd have to have a talk to them, to try and make them understand that they weren't free to publicise the fact that Adam came to their home in his free time. Although to be fair to her children, they didn't understand what Adam's occupation was because Dylan had chosen not to tell them. All they knew was that he talked like Superman and came from a place that was far, far away.

The drive home was completed in silence. The children had gone to sleep, leaving Dylan free to pursue her own personal thoughts about the last few hours.

"You're awfully quiet over there, Dylan, are you alright?" Adam inquired when he'd finally parked the car and turned off the engine. They sat in the car with neither one of them ready to make a move. It was a beautiful night. The heavens seemed alive with the brilliance of a million stars. Dylan was loath to move, she just wanted to sit there in the silence, with her thoughts.

"I was just thinking about tonight. It really brought matters home to me about how you're forced to live your life. It must be like living in a goldfish bowl. You really don't get much privacy, do you?" she declared, with uncharacteristic vehemence. She hadn't meant to sound so accusing, but the words had tumbled out of her mouth before she'd been able to censure them.

Adam chose to ignore the angry jibe, but told her instead, "It depends, tonight was nothing. I keep my private life to myself as much as possible, but you already know that. There are those times though when my life as an actor and my life as an ordinary person overlap. You and the kids won't have to worry, so please don't let it throw you. It's something you get used to after a while. Remember you won't be in the public eye so it won't concern you. You and the kids can lead a normal life away from it all. As far as you're concerned, I'm just an ordinary guy . . . ,"

"Who just happens to have a career making movies, working with glamorous females most of the time," Dylan interrupted, hating herself for her petty jealousy. Her voice sounded bitchy, even to her own ears. She didn't know why she asked the next question, it just seemed to pop out of thin air, shattering her normally lucid mind with its horrid implications, "Tell me, Adam, what do you do when females throw themselves at you, when all they want is to have sex with you? Do you push them away as easily as you did those people tonight?"

"Not always," the honesty of his answer shook her. It wasn't what she'd been expecting him to tell her. She looked at him through the darkness. He was looking out of the window, ignoring her presence. His face was set and rigid; he looked as if he was trying to hold his anger in check. Dylan could see by the small pulse that was beating at the side of his neck that it was hard for him to maintain a passive stance. His hands gripped the steering wheel in a vice-like hold that should have alerted Dylan to his dangerous frame of mind.

She was instantly sorry for this wall of silence that had been erected between them. She knew it was only there because of her jealous stupidity. "Adam," she said his name quietly, putting her hand on his thigh. She felt his instant reaction to her touch, but still he said nothing. Explaining the reasons for her outburst wouldn't be easy, but Dylan knew she had to try.

She began tentatively, "What happened tonight threw me. Like you said, you're used to it; it goes hand in hand with who you are, so to a certain extent you've grown to expect it. For me, it was a new experience. You say it won't affect the rest of us, but that's not entirely true. If we function as a family unit, there will be moments like tonight happening again. I expect I'll have to get used to it, in the future, but only because I have to, not because I must. I love you so, so . . . oh, what's the use. I'm not making any sense to me so how can I expect you to understand how I feel."

She made a move towards the door, feeling she'd somehow let him down when he'd needed her support, but not only that, she'd made a complete fool of herself in front of him. Adam's hand snaked out, stopping her before she could leave the confines of the car. He pulled her roughly into his arms, kissing her with a savagery that left her breathless. Dylan found herself responding, when, after a moment's hesitation she'd tried to pull away from him. She was lost and she knew it. She gave in to the raging passions assaulting her body; she was powerless to stop them.

"Is this how you think I behave when I'm not with you?" he demanded, his voice had a breathless raggedness about it that incited Dylan, not scared her. She knew instinctively that he wouldn't hurt her. Adam's mouth was ruthless as he plundered the sweetness Dylan offered to him willingly. His hands held her arms tightly against her sides, making movement impossible. "Do you think I chase after every woman who crosses my path . . . is that what you think of me, Dylan?"

Something within Adam told him to stop. He released Dylan abruptly, pushing her away to lean back trembling against the door. He was breathing deeply trying to regain some sort of control over his scattered wits. He couldn't look at Dylan, my god, what if he hadn't stopped! He felt sick. Guilt and shame rose up inside him; never before had he ever lost control in this way. He knew he had to face her, but what would he say to her. If ever he needed a script, he needed one now.

Dylan watched the play of emotions covering his face. She saw the disgust he was feeling and knew it was directed inwards towards himself and not at her. She wanted to help him so she searched her mind for something she hoped would make him feel less wretched; something to take the haunted look from his eyes. The words were there, waiting to be spoken.

"When you mix anger and passion, it can cause an explosive situation. We were both angry, Adam, both of us! Please, don't shut me out, talk to me," Dylan urged him tenderly, hoping her words would get through to him.

She wasn't sure if her heartfelt plea had reached him, but then he turned towards her to say quietly, "You're one hell of a woman, Dylan, do you know that?" He was thankful to her for helping him over an almost impossible barrier.

"Yes," she agreed with him, accepting the compliment. She saw a smile appear fleetingly on Adam's mouth, only to disappear again, "It's too late, I saw you smile," she teased him playfully, grateful for the small accomplishment.

"You're not going to let me feel sorry for myself, are you?" he asked defensively, looking over to where she sat silhouetted in the moonlight.

"No. No, I'm not," she told him truthfully. To prove her point, she moved closer to him and placed her lips over his in a light, but lingering kiss.

Her actions had the desired effect on him. Almost against his will, he returned her kiss. She was like a drug to him and he was completely hooked. Putting his arms around her, he held her closely. His body was trembling like a young boy's. He buried his head into her neck, just wanting to hold her, while he whispered quietly into her ear, "I'm sorry, Dylan."

Later, when the children were in bed, they settled down on the couch to talk over the events of the evening. She was saying to him, "I knew you'd stop. I had faith in your ability to do what was right."

"It's more than I knew," Adam told her truthfully. He was still shaken by his violent outburst.

"It's a good thing one of us is a good judge of character then, isn't it?" Dylan finally convinced him to put the last few hours behind him, saying it wouldn't do to dwell on it. She purposely changed the subject, telling him a bit more about her friends, Rae and Tom Burns.

"Rae reckons if we don't go around soon she's going to come around here and camp on the doorstep. I believe she's crazy enough to do it too. She's as whacky as a two-bob watch," Dylan mused thoughtfully.

"What?" Adam asked, quirking an inquiring eyebrow at her. He wasn't up on all of the Australian slang.

Dylan grinned, "I said she's good fun."

"I knew that," Adam feigned, knowing Dylan didn't believe him for a second.

"We'll have you eating vegemite yet, Yank," Dylan gurgled with laughter at the distasteful look Adam gave her at that remark. There were some things he just wasn't prepared to do, not even for Dylan.

Adam surprised her by standing up in front of her and with a flamboyant bow from the waist, he asked, "Would you like to dance, Ma'am?"

Standing up, Dylan gave a deep curtsy, putting her hand demurely into his as she did so, "Why, Mister Rossiter, I'd love to dance with you."

The music Adam had chosen was slow and dreamy. *Perfect,* Dylan thought as they circled the room, their arms lightly linked their bodies together. Dylan's head rested on Adam's shoulder while his head was supported by hers. They danced contentedly in this fashion, letting the music soothe them, the subdued lighting adding an element of mystery to the atmosphere in the room.

Dylan lost track of the time, she was happy to let the music flow around her. She felt happy; secure and loved as they swayed slowly to the beat; all of her apprehensions were forgotten for now. Their circles had become smaller until they were standing still. Adam moved his head from where he'd been resting it upon Dylan's head and brought his lips into contact with her ear, caressing the lobe gently with the tip of his tongue. Dylan felt her whole body ignite from this delicate touch and her body trembled with suppressed passion.

Turning her head ever so slightly, her lips met Adam's tenderly, invitingly. She planted small, sweet, wet kisses over his face before bringing her lips back to meet his. She put her whole heart and soul into the kiss she gave him, telling him with her body that she was his. Adam's body responded in kind. Dylan could feel his arousal, as she moved against him. She welcomed his ardent overture by putting her hands on his buttocks and blatantly pressed his body closer still to her own. Adam's hold on her tightened possessively as Dylan's soft breasts were pushed into his chest, forcing a groan of raw sensual emotion to escape from his throat. It heightened Dylan's senses, knowing she was the reason behind Adam's passionate responses. It was exhilarating to know this man shared her dreams and her passions for their future.

Wordlessly, they looked at each other, nothing needed to be said, it was all there in their eyes, and then in one easy movement Adam had her in his arms and was carrying her into the bedroom, their lips were fused together in a kiss that left her definitely wanting more.

Gently laying her on the bed, Adam quickly joined her, his hands fondling her breasts through the material of her dress. He could feel her nipples harden responding to his touch. Bringing his head down, he began to bite the swollen nubs, as they strained against the fabric that restrained them. Dylan's body shook convulsively with delight, loving the feelings that coursed unchecked throughout her body. Pin points of pleasure assaulted her as Adam weaved his magic over her.

Adam's voice came to Dylan from far away. She had to drag her mind back from the blissful fog enveloping her while she tried to concentrate on his words. Her body ached for him. Now wasn't the time for words, she tried to bring his hands back to her breasts, to recapture the exquisite rapture she'd been feeling. His voice penetrated her mind, it sounded thick and full of wanting. Looking up at him through eyes that refused to focus properly, Dylan's mind cleared enough to hear Adam saying, "Dylan, help me get this bloody dress off you. There's no zip or buttons and you're lying on it."

Seductive laughter gurgled up out of Dylan's throat as she obediently lifted herself so that the offending garment could be removed. In less than a heartbeat Dylan's dress was on the floor. Adam gazed down at Dylan's naked body as she lay waiting for him. She was so beautiful, everything about this woman excited him in a way that no other woman ever had. He loved her completely.

Dylan's own gaze travelled wantonly over Adam's magnificent torso, taking note of the way the hair on his chest curled around his small male nipples which, at the moment, resembled small hard buds. Her gaze then wandered down over his flat, firm stomach, down to his pelvic area where his manhood could be seen, erect and strong, waiting to complete their mutual, mounting desires. Dylan's kisses took her on an erotic journey as her lips travelled over Adam's body. His moans of pleasure became the catalyst for her emotions as she kissed and licked her way back up to his mouth, her hands roamed freely over him; she clutched him loving the hardness her hands encountered while her own body burned with a fire that only Adam could extinguish. She enticed him with her tongue, licking his lips erotically, before delving her tongue into his mouth to again taste his sweetness.

Adam's control was rapidly slipping; he could feel himself falling over the edge. Dylan had him at her mercy, he felt powerless to stop her. In one quick, fluid movement, he lay Dylan onto her back and then lovingly entered her body, forging himself repeatedly into her with firm masterful thrusts, giving her his love. Almost immediately Dylan felt her body exploding in a crescendo of passion. She couldn't stop the tremors that shook her to the very core of her being, as she reached the culmination of her heart's desire. She cried out blissfully, burying her head into Adam's neck, holding him tightly against her body as it shook uncontrollably.

Slowly, their breathing returned to normal. Adam held Dylan within the circle of his arms, gently kissing the side of her face. He brushed the damp tendrils of hair back from her face which exhibited all of the signs of freshly spent passion.

"Somehow just saying I love you after what we've shared doesn't seem enough. Every part of me belongs to you, Sweetheart. I'll always love you," whispered Adam.

Dylan felt a quiet contentment stealing over her. She felt she'd found her missing part and was now complete. She stated as much to Adam who answered affirmatively. A delicious languid feeling was slowly creeping throughout her body, so curling up against him, she whispered softly, "I love you," then almost immediately, she fell asleep.

Chapter Six

They had to be up early the next morning; Adam had to be back on the set by mid-morning. After a hurried cup of coffee, he was gone, waving to her as he drove away.

Dylan felt empty after he'd gone. She realised how much she'd come to rely on him for her happiness. Walking through the house, she looked for signs of him and was saddened when she couldn't find any, except for one lonely, black sock she found under the bed. What would it be like when they moved to America, when he was away on location for months at a time? *Like it is now,* Dylan thought. They hadn't discussed the situation to any great extent. Adam had wanted to, but Dylan kept putting the moment off, not wanting to think about it, much less talk about it. She knew that ultimately she'd have to face the facts that were before her, she didn't have a choice, not if she loved him. She decided what she needed was a breath of fresh air. Bundling the kids into the car, she headed towards Rae's place. Before too long, she was seated in Rae's big roomy kitchen with a cup of strong coffee in her hands.

"What's wrong with me, Rae? I've never been like this before. I've always been capable, able to manage my life. Even when Jake and I split up, I was able to cope, but now I feel so inadequate," Dylan finished lamely, as tears sprang into her eyes. She brushed them away angrily, too proud to let them fall. She stood up and began pacing around the room in a sudden burst of irritable energy.

Rae sat quietly watching her friend. She knew from past experience that once Dylan had mulled things over in her mind and had then talked her problems out, she'd be able to reach her own conclusions anyway, but Rae had to admit she hadn't seen her friend in such a quandary over a man before.

"I can't see the problem, Dylan. You say you love him and that he loves you," Rae's tone was compassionate, but firm, "Do you know how many women would love to be in your shoes right now? I'll tell you something, Dylan Miles, based on the facts you've given me, the man sounds besotted with you. So what if he doesn't ring as often as you'd like him to, or isn't around all the time. He doesn't exactly have a nine to five job now, does he?" Rae declared bluntly, trying to make Dylan see reason.

"Just how many women have been in my shoes?" Dylan flared, unleashing some of her anger at her friend. She continued to walk around the room, touching objects here and there, picking them up before she'd put them back in their place, unnoticed.

Rae shook her head, her eyes softening at her friend's obvious distress. "Past history, and might I add, does that really matter, he's with you now? Do you think he's judging you by the number of men you've been with in the past?" Rae knew this last remark was unkind, also, untrue. Dylan had only been with Jake before Adam. Rae was trying to make Dylan see reason. She continued, "If you plan to go on with him, you'd better smarten up or you'll lose him. What's more, it will be your unreasonable jealousy that drives him away and nothing else!"

Rae's comments produced a silence in the room while Dylan digested this last piece of information. Finally, she said, "I know you're right, of course you're right. I just can't seem to help myself. Maybe I should end things now and save myself the misery of a failed relationship later on. At least now I can walk away with a small shred of dignity still left in my possession."

Rae was staring at her incredulously. "You're serious, aren't you?" She felt drastic measures had to be introduced. It was time she cut in, to play devil's advocate or her idiotic friend was going to do something she'd end up regretting for the rest of her life.

She walked around the table, jerking Dylan none to gently out of the chair she'd just sat down on and then pulled her towards her bedroom. She wouldn't let go until she'd positioned Dylan before the large oval mirror which stood in the corner of her bedroom. Rae stood, hands on hips, all five foot four inches of her, her eyes blazing at Dylan who just stood there bewildered.

"Well, go on, look!" Rae demanded hotly, "Tell me, who do you see?"

"Rae, this is stupid. Who am I supposed to see?" Dylan asked impatiently, staring at her friend.

"You!" Rae stated calmly, keeping her anger in check.

"Me," Dylan was confused. *What was going on here?*

"Tell me who you see?" Rae repeated, insisting on an answer.

Dylan sighed, knowing the only way she was going to get out of here was to comply with her friend's wishes. She looked at herself critically, eyeing herself as she thought others saw her. *In comparison with the women she imagined Adam came into contact with she was downright dowdy,* she thought, *an everyday kind of person*

"I see an ordinary person who's trying to be Cinderella," she told Rae candidly.

"You would," scowled Rae, "You're a beautiful woman. That's why Jake won't let you go. You've got a good nature, good figure, kind heart etc., etc., etc."

"You make me sound like a horse."

"You're behaving like one, the rear end of one at that!" declared Rae, not to be put off, "Look, all I'm trying to do is stop you making the biggest mistake of your life. You've got a great guy in love with you and you're doing your best to destroy the relationship. Talk about being self-destructive!"

Rae brightened, as a thought struck her. "Do you know what you need? A night out with the girls! How long has it been since you've let your hair down?"

Dylan couldn't remember, "A while, I guess," *actually it would be nice to have a get-together with some of her friends,* she reasoned. She was warming to the idea, "Rather than go out, we could have it at my place."

"That's the spirit. I'll take care of it. I'll let you know when, you're just as likely to cancel out and believe me you need to relax, to enjoy yourself. A get-together with the girls can be fun, too, you know."

"I know. Just keep it small. You know I don't like lavish affairs," Dylan's mind automatically thought of Adam. There would be times when he'd need someone to act as hostess for him, if he entertained, or heaven forbid, walking the red carpet with him if he was expected to go to movie premiers, or the Oscars or whatever. She'd have to ask him. It was another piece of information concerning the life he led that she'd have to find out about. She secretly found herself wishing that she wouldn't be called upon to entertain the people he associated with in his role as an actor. She didn't voice these thoughts to Rae knowing her friend would have a logical answer to squash her doubts. Perhaps she was right. Dylan was erecting barriers she knew she wouldn't be able to climb when the time came.

Shortly afterwards, she left for home feeling completely washed out. The phone was ringing when she walked through the door. Glen picked up the receiver before Dylan could reach it. He'd developed the habit lately and she hadn't seen fit to discourage him.

"Who is it, Honey?" Dylan asked, as she put her things down on the kitchen table. The voice on the other end of the line had Glen captivated. He was smiling broadly while nodding his head, obviously agreeing, or liking whatever was being said to him.

"It's Daddy," he said, handing the phone to his mother before going down the hallway to his room.

Dylan frowned. Jake must have changed his ways for Glen to have responded so warmly. *Well, if he can be nice so can I,* thought Dylan, as she placed the receiver to her ear. She spoke casually, "Hi, Jake, how are you?"

Silence greeted her words. Her ex-husband was probably wondering what she was up to. She repeated playfully, "Come on, Jake, cat got your tongue?"

"It's Adam, Dylan," Adam's voice sounded curt and somewhat clipped, almost to the point of rudeness.

"Oh . . . I'm sorry. Glen said it was daddy," Adam's attitude puzzled her. She waited for him to continue. She loved the sound of his voice. The tone was so deep and vibrant. He sounded upset. Surely he wasn't angry over this little mix-up. Anyone could make a mistake.

"No, only me," He'd just confirmed Dylan's suspicions. "Actually, I'm ringing to tell you I can't make it this week-end. Some commitments I can't get out of concerning the movie," his voice sounded stilted, almost like he was holding himself in check. His voice was husky; Dylan thought his accent sounded more pronounced than usual. A sure sign something was bothering him.

"Adam," Dylan began, knowing she had to explain to him, "I thought you were Jake. I was being nice because . . . ," she wasn't able to say anymore. Adam interrupted her, saying he had to go. Dylan heard a voice in the background telling him to finish getting dressed, everyone was waiting. The voice was female.

"Tell your cousin good-bye, for goodness sake, Adam," Dylan heard clearly over the wires, "Come on, we've a party to go to."

"Well it definitely sounds like you're busy, so I won't keep you any longer," Dylan stammered. She felt her world crumbling around her. It seemed her instincts had been correct all along. If only she'd listened to them.

"Dylan!" his voice held a note of exasperation, "Don't hang up. I can explain."

Dylan replaced the receiver with trembling hands, feeling totally shattered. Cousin! The word rang in her ears like a claxon sounding the death knoll. They all think I'm his cousin and to think I'm the one who put the idea into his head in the first place. She half expected the phone to ring again; surely he'd try to reach her when he could with a perfect explanation for this awful fiasco.

As the hours slowly passed, Dylan knew she wasn't going to hear from him. She spent a restless night unable to sleep, finding that when she did dose off, her dreams were of Adam. He was with a faceless woman who called him darling; she was always just out of Dylan's line of vision. Adam laughed cheerlessly when she called out to him; he only seemed to be moving further away from her.

Dylan gave up any pretence of sleep. She'd rather be awake, anything was better than dreaming of Adam with another woman. She went out to the kitchen, perhaps a cup of herbal tea would help her to relax. Dylan hated herself for her traitorous thoughts. She must try to keep an open mind, there had to be a logical explanation. She owed it to any future they might have together to trust Adam before she condemned him without first hearing his side of the story. *There could be a very simple explanation to all of this,* she reasoned, as she sat down in front of the television.

Adam's voice woke her some time later. He sounded angry. Fully awake now, Dylan stared at the screen mesmerised by what was unfolding in front of her very eyes. A horde of reporters was hounding him. He was emerging from a well-known Sydney hotel surrounded by a crowd of people Dylan didn't recognise. One person in particular, a woman, had herself draped all over his arm. She was beautiful. Her figure was perfect and that dress . . . it clung like a second skin, a deep, rich red shimmering creation that showed every curve. She had long black hair that fell in thick waves down her bare back.

As much as Adam was trying to side step the press, this vision was manoeuvring him back into their path, into the path of the cameras. He looked wonderful in a tuxedo, so debonair and charming, totally belonging to this alien world Dylan knew nothing about, but one she was starting to hate.

Reporters were asking him a lot of questions about the movie which he answered curtly and with a lot of reluctance. He hadn't been kidding when he'd told her he hated giving interviews. One of the reporters, bolder than the rest asked him, "Would you like to tell the viewers who it is you visit every so often? Do you have any other interests over here at the moment?"

"None," Adam answered coldly, freezing the reporter with a frigid stare.

"We have it on good authority that you may be involved with a local lady," the reporter persisted. This would be a good story if he could get it.

Adam chose to ignore the question, trying to make his way to the waiting car. The same reporter pushed his luck a bit too far. He followed Adam to the car, determined to try once more.

"If you don't have any romantic interests with any of our local ladies, perhaps you can dispel the rumours that have been flying around Sydney lately about you and your lovely co-star here, Sara Longston. We've been told you two are a hot item at the moment. Are there any announcements you'd like to make to your adoring public, Mister Finlayson?" The young man was smiling, but not for long.

Dylan saw the fury building in Adam's face as she watched, totally horrified, unable to take her eyes away from the screen.

"Yes, just one. You can get f . . . ," the rest of Adam's speech was beeped out, but what was worse, he took a swing at the startled reporter. His fist connected with a sickening crunch with the man's jaw, sending him reeling backwards into his fellow reporters.

Someone from Adam's party came forward instantly to restrain him, in case he had any more dumb ideas. Dylan recognised the man as Simon Sutton. He was playing second lead to Adam in the film. Adam had told her Simon was a friend of many years, they'd worked together before. Adam was being ushered away into a car, away from the flashing bulbs of the cameras. Simon stayed to pacify the reporter who'd been hit. Dylan was pleased to see he seemed to be alright. Simon went on to tell the gathering crowd that he was sure he spoke for Mister Finlayson when he apologised for what had happened. He said Adam had been under a lot of pressure lately due to his responsibility on the set of the movie, so many things had gone wrong during filming. He was sure that an interview could be arranged whereby Adam could apologise in person, but for now he thought it would be best if everyone just went their separate ways.

The station went to a commercial break. Dylan sat there stunned, reliving the past few minutes in her mind. Why had Adam hit that man? Was he angered because it had been suggested he was seeing someone locally, or because he was having an affair with his co-star, or both? Which story was correct? Dylan knew at least one of the stories had an element of truth to it. He was involved with a local lady, herself to be precise. As for the other, she had no idea. Her worst fears had been thrown up in her face. Her future happiness was dangling by a very thin, very precarious thread. *All I can do is trust him and believe in him,* she thought. She wondered if there'd be any repercussions about his hitting the reporter. Also, she wondered if anything like this had ever happened to him before. She certainly hoped not on both counts.

The night passed slowly. Dylan saw the dawn break over the eastern sky as she sat forlornly on the back steps of her home, contemplating her future. The colours were magnificent, truly an artist's delight as the sun rose higher in the morning sky. She couldn't settle. She needed something to occupy her mind. Now was as good a time as any, she decided, to tackle her overgrown garden bed, the one she'd been putting off weeding for so long now. She dressed quickly in an old pair of shorts that had seen better days and an equally old T-shirt before donning a pair of headphones that were attached to her iPod and set to work, letting the music she'd chosen override her dulled senses. Even so, she found the gardening occupied her hands, but not her mind. The bouncy music couldn't budge the images of Adam that flashed through her mind of him with another woman.

Unknown to Dylan because of the headphones she wore, her phone was ringing. Adam was trying to reach her. Damn, he felt bad. He'd gone back to his hotel room with Simon after the producer's party last night, he'd ordered a bottle of whisky and between them, they'd drunk the lot. He was an ass. First, he'd been angry when Dylan had thought he'd been Jake, her ex-husband. There was no reason for her to have been so pally with the guy, was there? Jealousy was a new emotion for him and he didn't like it. Then, having to show up at that party and make out he was having a good time when all he'd wanted to do was to get in touch with Dylan to soothe things out between them. Sara had annoyed him all night, clinging to him, maybe before Dylan he would've been interested in the kind of affair she was hinting at, but not anymore. Acting with her was one thing, but anything else was out of the question. He'd find out who started the rumours about them, probably Sara herself, he conceded. She was a good actress, he admired her work, but that's where it ended for him. His heart was elsewhere and always would be. He just seemed to be having trouble convincing Dylan of that fact. This latest story, if it reached Dylan's ears would finish them for sure. He had to get to her first, to explain.

He'd had to promise that damned reporter an exclusive interview. Never before had he ever lost control of himself like that, regardless of the questions being asked. He'd never had so much at stake before.

Where the hell was she anyway, why wasn't she answering her phone? He had to go. He had an early morning call that he was already late for. He wasn't the producer's favourite person this morning, or the director's either for that matter. He'd try again later. He slammed the phone down angrily before leaving the room.

Rae arrived at Dylan's place a few hours later to confirm their get together, "They can only make it Thursday night, will that be a problem?"

"No, that's okay. Adam called last night, he can't make it this week-end, he's got some other commitment," Dylan told her friend warily.

"And?" Rae prompted, guessing there was more to it than she was being told.

Dylan glanced at Rae, what was the use of trying to keep the facts from her anyway. The awful story was probably plastered over some tabloid somewhere anyway. Rae might as well find out from her. Dylan told her friend what she'd seen.

"Mmm, I smell a rat. And he hasn't rung you since?"

"No," Dylan said flatly. She couldn't understand the highs and lows of her emotions. Yesterday, she'd been convinced leaving Adam was the only thing to do to preserve her sanity. Today, she was scared she was going to lose him to another woman. At least being in love with Jake had been something stable. She'd never felt this hurdy-gurdy roller coaster ride with him, her emotions had been fixed. When she was with Adam, she felt so alive; so sure of herself as a woman, but when they were apart, she lost all of her confidence and began to have doubts in herself and their relationship.

"If he's having an affair with his co-star, I doubt he'd want it to become public knowledge under the circumstances," Rae said almost to herself as she tried to work out all of the facts in her mind. She continued, "No, I think he's being set up. It sounds like this Sara person wants him; let's face it, Adam could do a lot for her career, couldn't he?" Rae assured Dylan, as she paced the floor stroking her chin with her slim fingers. She turned back to look pointedly at Dylan, "Do you know what I think?" Not waiting for an answer to her rhetorical question, she continued, "As I said before, I think this Sara person wants him for herself, but he won't give her the time of day. So she sets up this meeting with the press hoping it would make Adam realise she was around and available. Perhaps this was a last ditch attempt on her part. What do you think of my theory so far?"

"I think you're trying to make me feel better by clutching at straws. If you were right, why hasn't he tried to ring me to explain? If he cares so damn much, why hasn't he gotten in touch," Dylan felt the tears sting her eyes, as her voice started to falter. She quickly pulled herself together, showing some of her old spirit. It had been sadly lacking lately.

"Do you know what else I think? I think I'm making a fool of myself by hanging around waiting for someone who obviously has better things to do than ring me. No, Rae, enough is enough," Dylan told her friend, firmly slapping her hand down on the table when Rae would have interrupted, "it's time I did something positive for a change. Do you remember me telling you about that seminar the library wanted me to attend; well, I'm going to go. If I get a move on, I can still make it. My name's down for the second sitting. It's being held at Noosa on the Sunshine Coast. Mum has already said she'd take the kids if I decided to go."

"What if he calls and you're not here? I think you're wrong, Dylan," stated Rae bluntly.

"It won't be the first time, will it? Anyway, if he does ring he'll know how it feels to wait for someone. Let him be the one to feel the anguish, thinking you've lost someone you love. Let him feel it for a change," Dylan's hostile outburst fell on deaf ears. Rae wouldn't budge from her opinion, stating as much to Dylan as she prepared to leave.

"I hope you realise what it is that you're doing, Dylan. You could be throwing away a lifetime of happiness, all because you're too stubborn, or stupid, to realise what you've got," Rae threw at Dylan. Someone had to make her see reason.

"Then you stay here and wait for him. I've got better things to do," Dylan blazed hotly in defence of her actions. The one time she needed Rae's support, her friend was turning away from her.

Dylan just made the start of the seminar, sitting down just as the speaker walked into the room. She found she was interested in spite of herself and was soon caught up in the goings on around her. She purposely pushed Adam from her mind. This was the best thing she could have done, to get away like this.

The two days sped swiftly by and before she knew it, Dylan was returning home again. Only then did she let her thoughts of Adam over-run her mind once more. She knew this time away had been beneficial. She knew if need be, she could pick up the pieces of her life if Adam didn't return, however painful it might be for her to let him go.

Rae had told her she was running away, but Dylan preferred to think she was preserving her sanity. To sit waiting for a call that mightn't come would have finished her. This way, she could still go on hoping, believing, trusting in the man she loved. She hadn't the courage to stay and wait.

Rae had made Dylan promise she'd be back in time to entertain their friends. In spite of herself, Dylan enjoyed the time she spent with her friends. If she drank more than she usually did and perhaps wasn't as talkative as everyone else in the room, nothing was said. Dylan had asked Rae to keep silent about Adam, wanting to keep their relationship to herself. After all, there might not be a relationship to talk about anyway.

"Why don't I drive you ladies home? Your heads are going to be sore in the morning. You can leave your cars here and pick them up tomorrow," Rae suggested to the two women who were looking a little worse for wear.

"Are you alright to drive, Rae?" Dylan wanted to know, looking at her friend through eyes that wouldn't focus properly all of a sudden.

"Yes, I'm fine. I stopped drinking some time ago. Why don't you go to bed, I'll come back and clean up for you," Rae offered, smiling at her friend.

"No, I'll clean up. You can go home after you drop Beth and Tina off. I'm ok," Dylan responded and to prove her point, she stood up and started to clear away the mess.

"Stubborn till the end, aren't you, well, if you're sure," Rae still looked a little uncertain about leaving her friend, knowing the frame of mind she was in.

"Go on, or those two will start honking the horn soon," Dylan said, pushing her friend out of the door.

"Okay, I'll ring you tomorrow."

It didn't take very long to clear away the mess and wash the dishes. Dylan's earlier tiredness had vanished so she went into the lounge room where she poured herself another glass of scotch and thought back over the events of the evening. Looking at the contents of the liquid in her glass, Dylan knew she'd be sorry in the morning. Actually, this was very uncharacteristic for her; she hardly ever had more than two or three glasses at one time, if that, but if it helped her to forget the doubts whirling around inside her brain, why not.

Dylan thought sadly, *why am I so scared? He says he loves me, why can't I just accept it and be happy? Is it because I don't love him?* But as soon as this thought formed itself in Dylan's mind, she knew that wasn't so. It was because she loved him so much that she couldn't control her fears. *Look,* she reasoned with herself, *if you can fall in love so fast, so completely and so utterly, what's to stop the same thing from happening to him. Trust him,* her heart cried painfully, wanting an end to all of this misery.

"Yes, trust him," she answered herself out loud.

Dylan put on another CD and the words seemed to seep slowly into her alcohol filled brain. The song was an old one, it pulled at Dylan's heart strings. The tune was unashamedly sentimental, the singer told the world of his lost love, of his suspicions about his love and his subsequent heartache when she left him, never to return. The ambiguous meaning cut Dylan to the quick, releasing from her tortured mind vivid images of Adam and his svelte co-star. She had to try to lay her own suspicions to rest, or like the person in the song, she'd be left with nothing, but heartache.

Dylan felt the tears she'd been trying so hard to stop from falling since this horrible nightmare started, begin to fall, and once they started, she couldn't seem to stop them. She was past caring anyway. She gave in to the negative emotions which plagued her, needing to purge them out of her system. She was vaguely aware of a car pulling up outside, probably Rae coming back to check on her. At the same time, she was aware of a sick, dizzying feeling in the pit of her stomach and her head had started to spin in every direction at once.

Oh, no, don't let me be sick, please, Dylan thought frantically, as she made a mad dash for the bathroom where she knelt dejectedly over the toilet bowl and heaved her insides up.

At first, she wasn't aware of anyone behind her, but then a movement caught her eye and thinking it was Rae, Dylan wailed, between retching, "Rae, I feel terrible. How can people drink so much, if this is how they feel afterwards?" Another bout of nausea claimed her, so she lowered her head into the bowl again.

"It all depends on how much you drink," a familiar voice answered from somewhere behind her, but it didn't belong to Rae.

Dylan gave a loud groan and turned to see Adam leaning against the door, watching her. "Adam, what are you doing here?" Dylan managed to ask him.

"I was worried about you, and rightly so judging from the look of you. Do you want to tell me about it now, or wait until you sober up?" His voice held a hint of anger, but also something else, compassion. He was mad, but for some reason that Dylan couldn't fathom, he understood. At least she hoped he did. At the moment, she was too sick to care.

"There's nothing to tell. Some friends came over and we had a few drinks, that's all. Why should you be angry?" Dylan accused, looking at him again, seeing the grim lines around his mouth and eyes. Actually, he didn't look well himself. She continued waspishly, wanting to hurt him for the pain she was feeling, "If it's alright for you to go out on the town, I don't see why I shouldn't have some friends here. At least everyone here was female." Her body convulsed as another bout of nausea overcame her and she had to turn away from him.

He didn't try to help her in any way. "No, I guess not," was all he said, before he turned and walked away. Obviously, they needed to talk. Adam wanted some answers too. Like where had Dylan been for the last two days? He'd been frantic worrying about her, finally telling the director he was leaving for a day. He kept stuffing up his scenes anyway.

As Dylan washed her face, she could hear Adam in the kitchen, *probably making coffee to sober me up,* she thought, suddenly angry. "Well, he can stick his coffee," she muttered sullenly, as she turned on the water to the shower. She'd just started to undress when Adam came up behind her, taking her completely by surprise. He lifted her easily, putting her under the jets of water, clothes and all. Dylan was stunned. She stood there momentarily frozen to the spot. The look on his face, although not serious, was enough to tell Dylan what he was thinking.

I'll fix him, she thought, as an idea formed in her mind. Quick as a flash, she had her arms around him and had pulled him in with her. She had the satisfaction of seeing the water soak him completely, including his shoes as he struggled to get his balance.

"That's what you get for pushing me in. How do you like it?" she asked resentfully. Now that the deed had been done, she wasn't sure she should have carried it out.

Adam turned his back on her, so she couldn't see how the silly prank was affecting him. He was drenched from head to foot. His hair was plastered to his head and his shirt clung to his body like a second skin. He turned slowly, with rivulets of water still running off him. Dylan felt a quiver of excitement run through her body, making her shiver. She started to back away from him as he advanced towards her. The wall of the shower recess stopped her flight.

"Why did you do that?" he demanded, through clenched teeth.

"It seemed like a good idea at the time," Dylan declared defiantly, glaring at him.

"Where have you been for the last two days? I've been worried about you," Adam wanted to know, ignoring her sarcastic jibe.

"If you were so worried, why weren't you here two days ago? Or better still, I'll tell you, shall I? You were at some glitzy party with your glamorous co-star," Dylan still couldn't say her name. She continued, "You can't deny it. I saw you together on television. Tell me, did you hit that guy because of me, or her?" She was past caring what he thought. She needed to purge her mind of all the unanswered questions tumbling around inside her head. Not waiting for an answer, Dylan continued, "and why were you so nasty on the phone the other day, I don't understand." To her utter mortification, she broke down and started to cry.

Adam answered Dylan's last question first, "I guess I was jealous. You sounded so friendly when you thought I was Jake. It threw me." His voice sounded husky.

"Glen said it was daddy. He'd been laughing at something that had been said to him. I thought I owed it to the kids to be polite for a change," Dylan explained simply.

"Where have you been for the last two days?" he asked her bluntly, yet again. They were both oblivious to the water still streaming over them. It was more important for their questions to be answered.

"I was at a seminar. I mentioned it to you ages ago," Dylan enlightened him.

"That wasn't supposed to be on until the end of the month. Anyway, I thought you weren't going to go?" Adam remembered being told about the event, but they'd discussed it and Dylan had said it wasn't worthwhile attending if she was going to give her job up to go with him.

"The end of the month is now, Adam," she told him, glad at least that he'd remembered this small fact.

He looked disconcerted, as if he was trying to put things into perspective. "You could have let me know," He was looking at her steadily, willing her to answer him.

"How, by carrier pigeon? Anyway, you seemed to have your hands full," Dylan lashed out at him.

"Haven't we had this conversation before?" he asked wearily, wiping his hands across his eyes.

Dylan stubbornly wouldn't answer. She needed reassurance. She needed him to hold her, making the hurt go away. She didn't think that was too much to ask. The gap between them yawned widely and it seemed to be getting bigger all the time. This was a problem that had to be solved if there was to be any chance in the future for them. Dylan had to overcome her jealousy, she knew that. If only she could be sure. They needed to sit down and talk to each other, or their relationship was doomed to failure. One of them had to make the first move.

Adam clenched his jaw. He'd done all he could. He'd be damned if he was going to apologise when he'd done nothing wrong. Hopefully, Dylan would come to her senses and let him explain the circumstances surrounding the night of the party. He started to reach for a towel, why the hell was he still so wet?

"Adam," Dylan spoke so softly Adam almost failed to hear her. He looked back to see her looking at him, tears shimmered in her eyes. He raised his eyebrows at her, the only sign he gave that he'd heard her.

Dylan looked steadily at him, feeling very unsure of herself. "Hold me, please."

At first, Dylan thought he was going to ignore her plea. Then slowly, almost against his will, it seemed, he turned to her, indecision written plainly across his handsome features. A fleeting smile broke the sternness of his face, as he held out his arms to her.

Dylan stepped into them wrapping her arms tightly about his waist, saying to him over and over, almost like a chant, "Hold me, just hold me."

"Am I interrupting anything?" Rae asked innocently, making them jump guiltily apart.

"Rae!" Dylan looked at her friend, then back to Adam. How long had Rae been there? Had she heard any of their conversation?

"Correct me if I'm wrong, but I bet you're Adam?" Rae said, trying to keep the laughter out of her voice. She added, "Would one of you two idiots turn the shower off, or are you planning to stay there all night?"

"Oh, yes, right, the shower, Rae, what are you doing here? I thought you were going home?" Dylan stammered as she fumbled with the water tap.

"I drove past on my way home. The front door is wide open; just about every light in the place is on. I thought I'd call back to check on you, and what do I find? My best friend is in the shower, only partly dressed mind you, with a strange man." This last statement was her undoing. She dissolved into fits of laughter as she looked from one to the other of them. When she could finally speak again, she said, "I'm really going to enjoy hearing about this. Are you two ready to get out yet? I'll go and make us some coffee." Handing them a towel each, Rae said to Adam, "My name's Rae by the way, I used to be Dylan's minder until you came along. Good luck." They heard her chuckling all the way down the hallway.

"We'll never live this down you know that, don't you." Dylan told him, hoping his sense of humour would stretch to take in this outburst from her friend.

"I think perhaps you're right. Dylan, we need to talk about us," he sounded so serious, so determined and so final. Dylan was fearful. She thought she was about to lose him. The time had come at last. In a way, she was thankful, now she could get on with the rest of her life. The roller coaster ride was over. Dylan found she couldn't even cry. She had no more tears left.

"Come on," he said, as he helped her from the shower, "I don't know about you, but I could use a good strong cup of coffee right about now. Are you ok? You look like you're going to be sick again."

Dylan wasn't sure how she felt, but now that he'd mentioned it she did feel a bit queasy. She just made it to the toilet bowl before the retching started again. She joined Rae and Adam in the dining room some time later, feeling slightly worse for wear.

Rae looked up as Dylan entered, the smile she gave her friend belied her words, "You look terrible. You'll be sorry in the morning. Here drink this coffee."

Dylan sat in the vacant chair at the end of the table. She felt wretched and didn't care who knew it. The coffee tasted vile, but at least it stayed down. She was thankful for that small fact, at least. She felt so sleepy, her eyes refused to stay open.

She jumped with fright, when two voices told her simultaneously to go to bed. She opened bleary eyes, casting her gaze towards the two people who sat at the opposite end of the table.

"Off you go," Adam told her, "We'll talk later." He could have been talking to one of her children. His voice held no promises.

"She'll be sorry tomorrow," Rae smiled ruefully, feeling sorry for her friend, "It's completely out of character for her to behave like this. She's hurting. What are you going to do about it?" Rae didn't believe in beating about the bush, answers were needed and she intended to get them.

"If Dylan is hurting, it's because she won't trust me. She seems to think she's one of many. I can't convince her she's wrong. It's like talking to a brick wall."

"That's our Dylan all right. The trouble is you have another side to you that she isn't a part of. Why not invite her down south to see that side of things for herself or do you have something to hide?" Rae looked at him to see if he would take up the challenge she'd thrown down. He didn't bat an eyelid. Actually, he wondered why in hell he hadn't thought of it himself.

"Dylan told me you were straight forward," Adam told Rae wryly, before he answered the question that had been put to him, "No, I don't have anything to hide."

Rae glanced at him, deciding if she should tell him about her friend, "What has she told you about Jake?"

Adam felt his stomach muscles starting to tighten. He had a feeling he wasn't going to like what he was about to hear, "Nothing much. Only that he comes around from time to time, stirring up trouble. Is there any more to tell?" Adam wanted to know, he found he really wanted to know.

"Oh, yes, quite a lot in fact. His attacks weren't always verbal, you know," Rae told Adam about Dylan's life. She hoped it might help him understand her fears about committing herself to him.

Chapter Seven

The Sydney skyline looked very impressive as Dylan stood looking out of the hotel window as she gazed down upon the city that was sprawled out below her. The skyscrapers seemed to have multiplied considerably since her last visit to the New South Wales capital. The sun was sitting low on the horizon; lights were starting to come on all over the city. She had to admit it was a very impressive sight, but she also had to admit to herself that she preferred the quieter pace of Brisbane, but she knew that as a tourist destination Sydney was hard to beat. The harbour looked magnificent stretching for miles in any direction you cared to look. The Opera House was now alive with lights, standing elegantly beside the harbour. Its architecture was such that it resembled a fleet of large sailing ships whose majestic sails were billowing forth in full sail. Dylan had forgotten how beautiful this part of the country really was. She came to the conclusion that it would be exciting to refresh her memory of the city with Adam as her companion.

From her position on the exclusive hotel balcony, Dylan watched as thousands of cars made their way slowly across the harbour bridge. If she remembered her history correctly regarding the bridge, she was sure the bridge went from north to south across the harbour linking the two suburbs of Dawes Point and Milsons Point. She watched, fascinated, as the bridge came alive before her very eyes as thousands of strategically placed lights illuminated the steel structure, giving it a beauty it didn't possess during the daylight hours when its colour was a drab grey. Now, it had been transformed into a beautiful glowing ornament, stretching across the bay, shedding its magic light on all of the surrounding areas. Dylan was reminded of a wonderland as she watched the traffic move back and forth, across its girded magnificence. The total effect was very stimulating to the senses. She had an unfettered bird's eye view of most of the attractions that a tourist would find interesting. This week-end, if possible, she'd revisit them all.

Two weeks had passed since she'd seen Adam. He hadn't been able to get time away from the set to see her. They were working long hours, trying to make up for lost time. He'd suggested she come down to spend the week-end with him. He'd been so sweet, ringing her every day, sometimes late at night, whenever he'd had the chance. Dylan hadn't cared, just hearing his voice had been enough and then there was the flowers. He'd sent her several bouquets of carnations and roses. Dylan's house looked and smelt like a flower shop. She was back at work herself and was now very busy, catching up with her own work.

She'd just settled down with a cold drink, idly glancing through a magazine when she heard a key being turned in the lock. Adam opened the door and stepped into the room. He smiled warmly when he saw her. "Hi, Honey, been waiting long?" he inquired walking over to pull her gently to her feet, putting his arms around her casually, almost as though they'd only parted a short while ago. His actions belied his thoughts however, as he started to cover her face and neck with a quick succession of kisses.

"Have you missed me? Mmm, you feel good," he told her, savouring the feelings she induced in him. Two weeks was too long to go without touching someone you loved. He picked up the drink she'd discarded, taking a mouthful of the bubbling black liquid, while he waited for her answer.

"No, and yes," Dylan replied, grinning at him while he sorted out her replies into their appropriate sequence.

"Show me how much?" he ordered. His mouth flashed her a sexy smile, while his lively green eyes devoured her, bit by delicious bit.

"Yes, Sir," Dylan obeyed, giving him a mock salute, before stepping back into his strong embrace where she proceeded to kiss him thoroughly on the lips.

"That much," he whispered unsteadily a few minutes later fighting for breath.

Dylan's eyes were shining with unspent passion. She'd been eagerly waiting for this moment, too.

Adam reluctantly stepped away from Dylan's embrace. It would be too easy to lose himself in the delights of her body. He had other plans, at least for now. He hoped Dylan would understand and approve of them.

"Come on, Woman, enough of that!" he commanded, giving her one last quick kiss as he ushered her before him, towards the bathroom. He continued, "I made an early dinner reservation for us. I'll have a quick shower and then we can go down to the restaurant. Talk to me, while I get ready."

Sitting on the bathroom stool watching him as he showered, Dylan told him about her week, "It's been really hectic since I've been back. They've got me cataloguing all of the new books that have recently arrived."

"Sounds interesting," Adam replied absently, as he shampooed his hair.

"I think so," Dylan had to smile at his apparent total lack of interest.

Adam saw her gesture and shrugged his broad shoulders at her, by way of an apology.

Dylan enjoyed the novelty of being waited on and said as much to Adam after their dinner plates had been cleared away. She was feeling pleasantly tired and stifled another yawn as they sat leisurely drinking their coffee. It had been a long day; one Dylan had been looking forward to, for two whole weeks.

"Give me a home cooked meal anytime," Adam stated, reaching across to grasp her hand, "Come on, you're tired," he added, seeing her stifle yet another yawn. He wasn't any good at waiting.

Dylan was yanked to her feet and steered towards the doors of the restaurant that led to the lifts, "Adam, what's going on?"

"Nothing," he parried defensively, not quite meeting her eyes, "I thought we could have a quiet drink up in our room. You can relax there."

Dylan thought Adam was acting strangely, even for him, but she decided to go along with whatever was going on. Perhaps he only wanted to be alone with her. Dylan could relate to that. His nearness was weaving a spell over her, his after shave filled her nostrils and she breathed the aroma in deeply, loving the masculine smell of him.

"Here we are," he told her unnecessarily, as the lift glided to a smooth stop at their floor letting them out into their own private foyer. His smile held a boyish quality, but Dylan couldn't determine the source of his actions. She could have sworn he was nervous about something.

"Are you expecting anyone?" She asked at last. Maybe he wanted her to meet some of his friends. She felt something was about to happen.

"No. Why?" he answered defensively, putting the room card on the little oval table by the door. He touched the dimmer switch which controlled the lights and the room was immediately bathed in soft subdued light. A romantic setting if Dylan was any judge. "Go and put some music on, while I get our drinks ready."

Dylan chose some music that she particularly liked. She could see that he'd gone to a lot of trouble to make her feel special. Everything she could have wished for was right here in this suite of rooms. The music helped set the scene. She opened the drapes and a wonderland of lights greeted her eyes. It really was beautiful. She turned back in time to see Adam juggling a wine bottle, two glasses and a long box that was bound with a bright red ribbon tied in an elaborate bow.

"Come and sit down, I've got something for you," he said, patting the place next to him on the sofa.

How sweet, Dylan thought. *He's brought me a single red rose.* Love for this man welled up inside her as she made her way towards him. Nothing was as important to her as Adam right at this minute. He handed her the box with the rosebud in it, telling her to open it. His hand wasn't quite steady. She couldn't understand his nervousness. He'd given her flowers before. She knew the significance of giving a red rose, it was for love. He was telling her he loved her, using the symbol of the rose to say the words for him. She opened the box, feeling very special. The fragrance of the flower filled the room, adding to the romantic setting that already enfolded them.

Dylan almost missed it, the other box that was nestled between the folds of tissue paper. Her fingers shook as she removed it from its hiding place. Glancing at Adam, Dylan saw he was watching her intently. The smile on his face had been replaced by a more serious expression. He didn't say a word, but Dylan knew he was willing her to open the case. With hands that were no longer steady, she lifted the lid of the small box and quite literally gasped at what she saw there. Her free hand flew to her mouth and her eyes sought Adam's. She felt the tears gathering and was powerless to stop them falling.

"Do you like it, Dylan?" Adam asked. He seemed to be having difficulty with his breathing and took in a large lungful of air to steady himself.

Like it, she loved it. Lying in a fold of red velvet was the most beautiful ring she'd ever seen. One large centre diamond held pride of place and was surrounded by a cluster of smaller diamonds. The stones were set on a thick gold band.

Dylan swallowed convulsively, as she reverently took the ring from the box. "It's beautiful," she cried, the words catching in her throat, "Adam, it's beautiful."

She literally flung herself at him, kissing him with total abandon. Adam returned her kisses, showering her face with a barrage of kisses, matching his ardour to hers, before reaching down to take hold of the hand holding the ring.

"Put it on so we can make it official," his voice sounded gruff, even to his own ears. He cleared his throat. His eyes were suspiciously bright, also.

"I'd like you to do it," Dylan said, handing the ring to him. She held out her left hand to him and watched as he slowly slipped the ring onto her third finger. It fitted perfectly.

"You don't mind that we didn't pick it together?" Adam had agonised over choosing a ring by himself. He'd wanted to surprise her, hoping she'd approve of his choice. He knew some women considered diamonds to be old fashioned, wanting more exotic stones and settings, but for him it had to be diamonds. He was glad Dylan approved his selection.

"No, of course not, it's beautiful," Dylan told him again, as she gazed at the ring on her finger, loving the way it sparkled under the light. The weight of it felt strange on her hand. She walked out onto the balcony of their suite and stood looking down at the city sprawled far below her. It was now a hive of activity, just coming to life.

Adam came out to join her, putting an arm around her shoulder, drawing her closer to his side. "Happy?" he inquired softly, nuzzling her neck with his lips.

"Yes," Dylan nodded. There was no way around the question Dylan needed to ask, so taking a deep breath to fortify herself, she blurted out quickly, "Adam, will I be enough for you?"

Adam turned Dylan around so she could look into his eyes as he answered, "Lady, you're too much. I feel like I've been flattened by a truck, you knock me out." He lowered his lips to hers, proving his point. Lifting his head sometime later, he murmured huskily, 'Satisfied?'

"Not entirely," Dylan croaked throatily, bringing his mouth back down to hers. Her whispered, "Never," was nearly lost to him as their mutual desires mounted.

Adam watched Dylan as she slept. She looked so vulnerable, making him feel protective towards her. He gently brushed some fine strands of hair from her eyes. It was in its usual curly disarray and instantly sprang back from his fingers, causing Dylan to frown slightly in her sleep. Her fingers moved fleetingly over his stomach, feeling for him before she drifted back into deeper slumber once again.

He was content. They'd cemented their relationship tonight when Dylan had accepted his ring. Surely now she'd realise he was totally committed and wanted nothing more than to settle down with her and their respective families. Maybe they'd even have children of their own one day, he'd like that. He smiled ruefully, if anyone had suggested to him six months ago that he was about to meet the woman of his dreams, he would have laughed at them. Rae had been right when she'd told him Dylan needed something tangible to make her realise he was serious. Jake had really dumped on her, according to Rae. Adam felt cold anger rising within him, as he recalled some of the things he'd been told. It was a wonder Dylan's emotions had ever recovered from the scarring they'd received at the hands of her ex-husband.

Adam had to leave for the studio at four in the morning, so he was up and gone before Dylan had woken up. He'd left a reminder of himself for Dylan to see when she opened her eyes. The single red rose was lying on his pillow with the hastily written words, 'I love you' secured to the stem.

Adam had arranged for someone to pick Dylan up later in the morning to escort her to the studio where filming was in progress. She had a leisurely bath, pampering herself, using the scented bath salts she found in the back of the bathroom cabinet. *This place caters for everything,* Dylan thought as she stepped into the fragrant water. Her skin had started to pucker like a prune when she finally decided it was time to get out of the tub. Adam said not to dress up, telling her to wear something she'd be comfortable in. Out came her jeans and sneakers plus a T-shirt belonging to Adam that she decided to put on at the last minute.

Walking through the studio doors was like going into another world. Everywhere Dylan looked, there was something happening. The words that instantly sprang into her mind were 'confusion' and 'chaos'. How could something as wonderful as a movie come out of all this clutter?

Dylan's guide asked someone if he knew where Adam was and they were waved off in the direction of a trailer that was situated at the rear of the massive building. Silence greeted the knock on the trailer door, so Dylan was left to wait. Her guide, who had introduced himself as Joe, told her he was a runner. Dylan didn't have a clue who, or what, a runner was, so she just smiled pleasantly and kept her mouth shut, not wanting to show her ignorance.

"Adam probably won't be long. He'll be roaming around the place somewhere. He sent me to get you so he's expecting you. Make yourself comfortable, if you'd like to go inside there you'll probably find some coffee and maybe something to eat. You'll have to excuse me, but I have to go," Joe told her, already making his way towards another group of people, who seemed to be calling for his assistance.

Dylan sat down on the steps of the trailer, content to watch the goings on around her. She was fascinated by everything she saw. There were racks of clothing standing in one area, each one had the name of a character from the movie attached to it and in another area make-up was being applied to a group of people, probably getting them ready for the day's shooting, other areas had been set up to depict certain scenes from the actual movie. As for the rest of the equipment, lights, cameras and cranes, people were manning them manoeuvring them into position ready to be at the director's beck and call. There was a sea of other people who seemed to be wandering around the large sound studio, each one bent on performing a different task that would ultimately go towards bringing all of this magnificent chaos to life. Dylan found it all terribly interesting. She found herself wondering yet again how Adam could perform as naturally as he did in front of the bevy of people and cameras that were being readied for the day's shoot. It made her realise, yet again, just how far apart their backgrounds really were.

Searching the sea of unfamiliar faces, as they busily moved around her, she looked for Adam, but couldn't make him out anywhere. She finally noticed a man heading towards her and felt her stomach muscles start to contract as she recognised the man she knew as Simon Sutton.

"You're Simon Sutton!" she told him excitedly, then immediately felt foolish, as she felt a tell-tale blush creep up her neck and settle on her flushed cheeks. He'd think she was acting like an overgrown groupie.

"Yes," he smiled, "and I bet you're Dylan." He held out his hand to her. Dylan didn't hesitate about returning the gesture, liking this man instantly. He was handsome in his own special kind of way, having thick blond hair and incredible blue eyes that reminded Dylan of a cloudless summer day. He was not as tall as Adam, but Dylan would have bet money on his popularity with members of the opposite sex. He had a definite 'boy next door' image that she knew the girls would go for in a big way.

Engrossed in conversation with Simon, Dylan didn't see Adam approach. She was laughing at something he'd told her and was therefore startled when his deep voice whispered in her ear, "Hi there, remember me?"

Dylan's face lit up with pleasure at the sight of him, a fact which pleased Adam greatly. He bent down to lightly place a kiss on her lips.

"Adam!" She blushed slightly, "I didn't see you come in."

"I noticed. Has Simon been looking after you?" he inquired, as he took a seat next to her on the trailer step.

"Yes, he's been the perfect host," Dylan told him happily, glancing across to look at Simon.

"That's what worries me," Adam said, throwing his friend a cautionary look.

"This little lady wouldn't have anything to do with the temper tantrums the 'star's' been throwing lately, would she?" Simon already knew the answer. He'd bracketed the word star with his fingers as he'd said the word, giving it the emphasis he'd wanted.

Adam had the grace to look away sheepishly, confirming his co-stars suspicions. His healthy, tanned face turned to a ruddy hue, causing Simon to remark with satisfaction, "So," he said, satisfied with his assumptions, "The great lady killer has been brought down . . . about time too."

"Get out of here," Adam grinned, while watching his friend stroll casually away.

"Temper tantrums?" Dylan speculated idly, running her fingers along his arm in a casual caress.

"Everyone needs a hobby," Adam defended his actions with a shrug of his shoulders, not quite able to hide the grin that had manifested itself on his handsome features.

Dylan gave him a quick hug, "So tell me, when does the action start?"

"Pretty soon, actually, I have to go over to make-up and wardrobe. Come on, you can come, too," He stood up, pulling Dylan along with him, "It's time for the big transformation."

"Love your shirt," he declared casually as they walked towards the make-up trailer.

Dylan sat awe struck as Adam was transformed from the man she knew and loved into a virtual stranger right before her eyes. He was fitted with a long hair piece that matched his own shiny brown locks, before being further transformed with the addition of some rough looking facial hair and thick fluffy side burns. The whole effect was overwhelming to Dylan who felt like she'd fallen down a rabbit hole and was now securely entrenched in Wonderland. Everything held her interest. She didn't need to pinch herself, reminding herself of the reality of her surroundings, but at the same time everything around her was steeped in reality. Simon was there also, having his make-up applied along with some other members of the cast.

Out on the set, Dylan saw first-hand why Adam had earned his reputation as an excellent actor. He worked well with the director, sometimes suggesting different ways of doing something which he thought would work in a particular scene. Sometimes the director wasn't happy with the performances of his stars and would want the scene to be redone. Dylan was surprised to see that it happened on a regular basis. Actually, to give Simon his due, he wasn't all that bad either, Dylan conceded. She was totally engrossed in the action taking place in front of the cameras. It was so easy to lose one's self in the reality of it all, from a bystander's point of view. Adam had told her that they only got through three or four pages of script a day, depending on what had to be done. Some parts of the movie had been shot in various other locations including the Blue Mountains area which was west of Sydney.

In the scene being shot now, some troopers had Adam pinned down and it looked as if his ultimate capture was imminent and that would mean his death. Simon's character was supposed to creep in from behind, trying to help Adam escape, but unknown to them both, troopers had crept around behind them, and they were trapped. In the ensuing scene, Simon was to be shot. Dylan was so completely engrossed in watching the scene unfold before her that she forgot where she was and she yelled out wildly, when she heard the fatal gunshot, "Watch out, Simon!"

Instantly, she realised what she'd done. Everyone stopped to stare at her. She could feel herself blushing madly and secretly wished the ground would open up and swallow her, taking her embarrassment with her. Looking across at Adam, she could see he was grinning broadly. Simon was trying very hard not to laugh; he was covered with fake blood that looked very real to Dylan's untrained eye. In the end, he gave up and laughed uncontrollably, along with everyone else.

She turned to the director, feeling very foolish, "I'm really sorry, honestly, I am. I got carried away."

He, too, was smiling Dylan noticed thankfully, "No permanent damage done. It's nice to know our work is appreciated," then to everyone he said, "Ten minute break, okay."

Adam had come to stand by her side. He commented, "You're lucky you got him on a good day, otherwise he'd bite your head off."

"Thanks," she answered dryly, digging him playfully in the ribs, "You don't know how happy that makes me feel."

Dylan was surprised when a short time later, Sara Longston walked onto the set. She recognised her from various movies she'd seen the actress perform in. She was more beautiful in the flesh, even with minimal make-up as she appeared now. She walked up behind Adam, putting her arms possessively around him, before pulling his head down to kiss him on the side of his face.

"Hello, Darling, are you ready for our scene together?" Then she turned to Simon saying, "Simon, do you think we could go over those lines of yours? I don't want to be stuck here again all day." Then turning back to Adam she said, "Adam, can we go to that little place down near the Rocks for dinner, again? It was so quaint."

Dylan felt her insides tighten as she listened to the woman's monologue. She forced herself to stay calm, not by one false action did she indicate her true feelings as she sat there. She looked at Adam, wondering what his reaction would be to his co-stars brazen invitation.

He extracted himself from Sara's embrace and looked across to Dylan, willing her to believe that this attraction that Sara had towards him was completely one sided. She smiled and even managed to give him a wink, but could she help it if the warmth of her smile didn't quite reach her eyes.

"Do you mind, Sara. You're going to give my fiancée the wrong idea," To Dylan he said, "Honey, this is Sara Longston. She plays Mabel Smith. The entire cast ate at the restaurant after shooting the other night, that's all."

Sara turned to look at her and Dylan saw the raw hate that was aimed in her direction. "Your fiancée . . . is that what you're calling them, these days? Well, let's hope this one lasts longer than the others. You do seem to pick the plain ones, don't you?" She turned and walked to one of the make-up chairs where she sat down, quite unperturbed by the bombshell she'd just dropped in Dylan's lap.

Dylan was fuming, but she swore she'd cut her throat before she uttered one word to that viper. When she had herself under control, she said pleasantly to Adam, "Testy little thing isn't she? Must be P.M.S. It gets some women that way."

"You don't believe that garbage do you?" Adam protested, looking bluntly at her.

"No, no, of course not. I know jealousy when I see it." Now wasn't the time, or the place to discuss this. Dylan's brain was numb. She refused to think about it now.

"For what it's worth, Dylan, Adam is telling the truth. We were all there, ask anyone." Simon stated, hoping he could help ease the situation between them. Sara could be vicious when she was stalking a man she wanted. She had no scruples when it came to moralising over anything she did, or said.

Dylan touched the diamonds sparkling on her finger, making herself remember the commitment they'd made to each other. *No one could be that good an actor, could they? That passion had been real; please, God, that passion had been real.* She took a deep breath, before saying calmly, "I know."

Adam visibly relaxed. He'd been holding his breath. *So much for a pleasant afternoon,* he thought miserably. If he lived to be a thousand years old, he doubted if even then he'd be able to understand women.

The next few hours for Dylan were miserable ones indeed. She spoke when spoken to, smiled on cue; she even managed to laugh now and again. On the outside, everything was fine, but inside, she'd shrivelled up. If Adam noticed her withdrawal, he said nothing to enlighten her. Before Adam had to do his scene with Sara, Dylan made an excuse to leave. Nothing short of being tied to a chair with her eyes stitched open with string would induce her to stay and witness the two of them kissing, even if it was only part of a script.

"Are you sure? I won't be long now," Adam told her. He'd guessed her reason for wanting to leave. He'd really wanted her to stay, so she could see for herself how a love scene was done. The actors involved were always at the director's discretion, being told to move either this way or that; to do this or that and so on. He wanted her to see that feelings didn't come into it when actors did a love scene. It was purely mechanical, but short of causing a scene, he was powerless to stop her.

"No, I'll go now and see you back at the hotel," Dylan stood passively, while Adam kissed her and then turned to leave. She hoped she'd be able to get a taxi once she found her way outside.

"Hold on, then, I'll walk you out," Adam told her only to be stopped short by the director, telling him they were ready to roll.

Adam swore under his breath, before he said again, "Look this won't take long."

Simon stepped in, saying to them, "Go do the scene, Adam, before Sam has a coronary. I'll see Dylan out."

Adam looked uncertainly at both of them, but was called again, more persistently this time. "Ok, I'll see you later," he told them, as he spun on his heel and walked over to take his cue next to Sara.

Once they were outside, Simon led Dylan to a waiting taxi, "That was a pretty good performance you put on today. An Oscar winning role if ever I saw one," Simon commented to her, as he ushered her inside the cab. On impulse, he bent down to give her a quick kiss on the cheek.

Dylan didn't know why she stayed. If she had any sense, she'd leave now. The only trouble was, she'd been wrong before. Adam deserved to be able to tell his side of things. Simon had said they were all there at the restaurant. All of this evidence was damning to be sure, but it didn't add up. Why would he have gone to the expense of buying her a ring, if he wasn't serious?

Dylan sat alone on the sofa, gathering her thoughts about her. Her mind returned to the day's events once more and settled on Sara Longston. She would never admit having done this to Adam, because she knew what his reaction would be, but after her last bout of uncertainty when she'd thought he'd been unfaithful with Sara Longston she'd googled him wanting to know if he'd had any romantic connection with her in the past. She's been relieved to find nothing connecting them. She'd hated herself for doing it, but her motives had been driven by jealousy towards the other woman. His name had been linked with others though; a fact that she hadn't particularly liked, but she was quick to tell herself that was before he'd even known of her existence, so in fairness to him she had dismissed them. She was relieved to see that he hadn't been overly serious with anyone because his affairs, she had cringed at that word, hadn't seemed to last very long. It appeared that as soon as he finished with one woman he was reported to be with another one. The information backed up his claim about the meaningless affairs he'd been involved in. He'd told her that most of the time these women were only with him to further their own careers saying it wasn't always him that did the chasing. He'd been honest in that regard. She found herself wondering yet again what he saw in her when she thought of the high profiled, not to mention beautiful women he'd known before knowing her. *Photographs don't lie,* she reasoned as she'd looked at the long list of women that he'd been involved with over the years.

Darkness was falling on the world outside, but Dylan's thoughts were still entrenched in the past. She couldn't be bothered getting up to turn on the lights, so she sat there surrounded by the gathering darkness.

Her thoughts continued to haunt her throwing her back into the past. Fate must have wanted them to meet, it must have been preordained, fate was said to move in mysterious ways and she believed that to be true. If it hadn't been for the wrong turn he'd taken while driving back to Brisbane after a day spent sight-seeing at the Sunshine Coast, a turn that had ultimately brought him to her isolated part of the world and added to this was the fact that hers had been the only house showing lights on that particular night they would never have met. Dylan would never have come to know the wonderful man she had fallen so completely in love with. The ordinary man who lived behind the facade of stardom.

Adam arrived back at their suite some time later, to find the rooms in total darkness; it made him feel uneasy. "Dylan," he called softly, walking towards the bedroom, perhaps she was sleeping. He could smell the lingering scent of her perfume and breathed deeply, loving the image the aroma presented to him, but it seemed that the vibrant scent was all that was left of her as his eyes scanned the empty room that greeted him. He cursed loudly and then sat down heavily on the bed to gaze unsteadily at the wall. *Why was it always like this?* He was beginning to wonder if being in love was worth the effort. Would he go after her this time? Perhaps it was better to let things lie. But as soon as the words formed in his mind he knew them to be untrue. He would go after her because she was a prize worth fighting for. He would convince her that she was the love of his life if it killed him.

"Adam," He jumped off the bed upon hearing his name, turning to face Dylan. She was standing in the doorway looking at him.

All condemning thoughts were forgotten as he strode towards her and gathering her in a strong embrace, he rocked her gently back and forth, while telling her softly, "I thought you'd gone."

"I very nearly did," she answered him truthfully and was immediately pulled closer to his hard body.

"What made you stay?" he muttered against her hair, breathing in the smell of her.

"Because as strange as it may seem, I love you, the things that were said today didn't add up, and once I was able to think clearly I could see the loopholes in Sara's story," Dylan could feel the tautness in his body, so pushing him back down onto the bed, she began kneading his shoulders and neck in an effort to free him from the tension she'd felt building up inside him.

"That feels so good," he sighed, bringing his head back to rest against Dylan's ribcage. He closed his eyes, enjoying the sensation of being administered to by her capable hands.

"I enjoyed today," she told him, making casual conversation. *Well, most of it,* she added silently.

"Good, that's good," he answered absently, giving himself up to the soothing sensations that had started to permeate throughout his body.

"I could have said I stood naked in the lobby and I'd still get the same answer, wouldn't I?" Dylan's tone was gentle, her touch soft. He was almost asleep.

"Mmm," he whispered, proving her point beyond a doubt.

She smiled, not at all put out that he had his selective hearing ears on. It had been a long day for both of them one way or another. They could talk later. She lay down next to him and within a few minutes they were both asleep.

The following morning, Dylan was sitting on the sofa leisurely reading a women's magazine. She'd just finished doing a quiz when Adam walked through from the fully stocked kitchen that was a part of his suite of rooms.

Asking casually, as she looked at him over the top of the glossy magazine, she enquired "Adam, do you think we're too physical? According to this quiz, we are."

Adam just about choked on the spoonful of ice-cream he'd put into his mouth. He was staring at Dylan like she was demented.

"What!" he spluttered, as he grabbed a towel from the chair to wipe the cold confection from his face.

"I said . . .,"

"I heard what you said," he returned, coming to sit down beside her and grabbing the magazine from her hand, he started to scan the page and its contents.

"This was probably written by a nun," he joked, handing the article back to her, "Personally, I don't think we get physical enough."

"According to this article that is a typical male response," Dylan told him smugly, waving the glossy pages under his nose to re-enforce her statement.

"Is that so," he declared, bringing his lips into contact with her neck, nuzzling the sensitive spot under her ear, sending shock waves throughout her body from his casual caress. Her nipples hardened beneath his expert touch.

Dylan tried to squirm out of his embrace which only made him more determined to hold her. "That's not fair," she declared, "I wasn't expecting you to do that."

"Excuses, excuses, nothing but excuses," he taunted, knowing exactly the reaction his touch would invoke in her.

"I bet you couldn't sit there calmly while I did something like that to you," Dylan replied, defending her body's reaction to his casual caress.

"Go for it," he challenged, clasping his hands behind his head, giving her free access to his body.

Dylan was slow and thorough as she went about her task, touching him, tantalising him; using every ounce of womanly wile she possessed to arouse him.

It took every ounce of strength and restraint Adam possessed to appear untouched by Dylan's actions. Smiling to herself when she noticed a fine sweat had broken out on his brow and upper lip, Dylan decided to change her tactics and stopped suddenly.

"Okay, you win," she conceded defeat magnanimously, hopping up from the sofa to make her way casually towards the balcony. She'd give him till the count of ten to make his move.

"Hey, you weren't supposed to stop," His voice held a slight tremor that he couldn't quite control. He jumped up to follow her outside.

"Seven," Dylan said, satisfied with her calculations.

"Seven what?" Adam asked, thoroughly confused by her strange statement.

"Oh, never mind," she smiled sweetly up at him, "Just a private thought I had. I'll just go and get ready to go out. Won't be a tic," she added casually.

"Dylan!" he groaned at her pleadingly, drawing her close to his heated body.

"Are you willing to accept defeat?" Dylan inquired, scrutinising his taut features. He was ready to fold.

"Yes," he groaned, giving in gracefully, as he moulded her to the contours of his heated body. All thought of talk was forgotten as their desires mounted. By mutual consent, they walked into the bedroom where the rest of the world was temporarily forgotten.

Adam brought his lips down to make contact with Dylan's breast; he felt her shudder delightfully in response. She pressed his head closer, arching herself into him. The hardness of his body inflamed her, as she felt his nearness. He took her slowly, kissing all of her, until he had her writhing with uncontrolled passion. She burned with an insatiable hunger; her body seemed to be unquenchable when it came into contact with his. Her softness melted under the expert guidance of his hands, as he weaved his magic over her. Her body felt like a volcano ready to erupt, liquid red hot fire seemed to be coursing through her veins, turning her into a mindless fool with only one thought on her mind . . . possession. She guided him inside her eager, waiting body and then wrapped her legs around him, trying to draw him closer still. They moved together as one, their minds and bodies in complete harmony. Dylan felt her body moving towards its ultimate goal and so gave herself up to the rapturous, frenzied desire that carried her headlong over the precipice where mind, body and soul became one. She exploded with a crescendo of fireworks, taking Adam with her on a journey of exquisite pleasure. She sank her teeth blissfully into his neck, totally unaware of doing so. Adam rested the top half of his body on his elbows, to take his weight off Dylan, while his lower half still covered her like a protective blanket. He kissed her lovingly, gently, until their breathing returned to normal.

They spent the rest of the day wandering around Sydney. They strolled through Kings Cross, which was now strangely quiet. Kings Cross was a hive of activity during the night time hours, but during the day, it reverted to a place of subsequent quietness. Their wanderings brought them to Circular Quay where they took a ferry ride to Manly. Dylan was secretly relieved to get back onto firm ground. They watched the hydra-foil skim over the surface of the harbour. There was an open air concert at the Opera House, but they declined to stay, preferring to keep moving.

Dylan was peacefully happy and content to amble along, arm in arm with Adam, looking through the different shops that were open on this glorious Sunday afternoon, obviously to attract the tourist trade. Adam bought the boys and Natalie a gift each, arranging for them to be delivered to the hotel, for Dylan to take back with her.

A short time later, Adam rubbed his stomach. "Are you hungry? I just realised we haven't eaten yet. There's a place over there. Come on, I'm starving."

Until he'd mentioned it, Dylan hadn't felt particularly hungry, but now realised that she could eat something. They decided to eat their food in one of the parks that skirted the harbour.

Adam had chosen hot dogs, while Dylan thought she'd wanted pizza, but looking at Adam eating his hot dog which he'd smeared with mustard and sauce, she felt a definite craving for his lunch, "Can I have some of yours, please? It smells really good."

Adam held his food against his chest, "I thought you wanted pizza? Isn't it just like a woman to change her mind," He looked mournfully at his second hot dog before handing it over to her, "Do you want my soda, too?" he added, as an afterthought.

Dylan pretended to think about it before telling him, no, she was happy with the one she had.

They were acting like a couple of kids, swapping their food and generally enjoying the tranquillity of their surroundings. From where they sat, they commanded an excellent view of the harbour. They watched as a large passenger liner made its way slowly towards the heads, while they debated about where they thought its final destination would be.

Adam lay down on the grass with his head resting in Dylan's lap. She ran her fingers through his hair, loving its soft texture. Looking around her, she could see other couples were taking advantage of the excellent weather Sydney was having. In fact, one or two couples were quite blatant in showing their affections for each other.

Her gaze focused on Adam and she was surprised to see him grinning up at her, before he looked over at one young couple, who seemed to be oblivious to everyone and everything around them. He pulled Dylan down until she was stretched out along the length of him.

"Why should they have all the fun," he stated, bringing his lips into contact with her own.

"If you think I'm going to provide a side show for the rest of the locals, Sport, you can think again," Dylan told him, trying to suppress the giggle that was bubbling up within her.

"No one's going to notice us. Look around," he told her knowingly.

Dylan had to admit he was right. It seemed they'd stumbled into the local lovers' playground. She had a thought and glanced at him accusingly, "Did you know about this place?"

"No," He cast her an injured look that held just a touch of mischief, "But why waste the experience. Now shut up and kiss me."

Dylan did as she was told and was instantly caught up in the madness that surrounded them. Self-conscious, at first, she was slow to respond, but was soon intoxicated by the heady feelings that overtook her whenever they kissed.

They were soon brought back to earth by a tap on Adam's shoulder and a humorous voice, vaguely familiar telling them, "When you two come up for air, maybe you'd like to go somewhere just a little bit more private than a public park."

Looking up through passion glazed eyes, Dylan was horrified to see Simon grinning down at them and as reality returned to the emotional fog she laughingly called a brain, she felt her cheeks burning from the soft flush that stained them. Glancing at Adam didn't help, because, although he seemed to be somewhat subdued, he was otherwise guilt free. *Possibly due to his training as an actor,* Dylan thought, getting unsteadily to her feet. She wished the ground would open up and swallow her. Looking around her, she was pleased to note no one else had seemed to notice their impropriety. *Thank goodness for small mercies,* she thought gratefully, running shaky fingers through her hair. She caught Adam's eye again, letting him know by her woeful look that he hadn't heard the last of this. He gave her a rueful smile in return, before turning to listen to what Simon was saying.

"If you ever need a stand-in, Adam, you can call on me . . . please."

This statement had Dylan blushing again, while Adam told his friend, and co-star, "I don't need a stand-in Simon, I do all the hard stuff myself; you know that."

"Lucky you," the other man declared, winking at Dylan.

Adam caught this gesture as the three of them started walking along the path, leading to a more populated part of the park.

"Hey, find your own girl and go and flirt with her," he quipped, cuffing Simon playfully on the chin. He held up Dylan's left hand where the diamond ring sparkled brightly and then added, "This one's taken."

Later, back at their suite, Dylan was able to laugh about the events of the afternoon. She'd just showered and was now packing her case ready to catch the late flight back to Brisbane. Adam was lounging on the bed, lazily watching her. She looked at him thoughtfully, before asking, "I wonder what would have happened if Simon hadn't have come along?"

"Oh, I don't know. I guess someone would have thrown a bucket of water over us," he answered her with a mischievous glint in his green eyes.

"You're impossible, do you know that?" Dylan teased, coming to stand at the foot of the bed. She took one of his feet in her hands, absently caressing his toes, while she gazed at him. They only had a few short hours before they'd be apart again and the loneliness and the missing him would start all over again.

"But you love me anyway?" he asked her, trying unsuccessfully to ignore the sensations shooting through his body caused by Dylan's casual caress. His arousal became painfully obvious to them both and Dylan's sharp intake of breath, as she drank in the sight of him was no more than a low guttural sound from somewhere deep in her throat.

"Yes, I love you anyway," she answered hoarsely and shedding her robe, climbed onto the end of the bed from where she proceeded to make her way on her hands and knees up and over the length of him moving slowly and provocatively. Her mind registered hearing his sharp intake of breath as her body came into contact with his. The fabric of his clothes, rubbing against her body proved to be an intoxicating stimulant. Her breasts became taut and her womanly core flooded with desirous moisture. She made herself the instigator in their game of love, leading Adam down a passionate trail fraught with unimagined delights for both of them. Her breathing became ragged, as she continued her onslaught of his body.

"Dylan . . . dear god . . . you're incredible," Adam managed to gasp. He'd reached the limits of his endurance. A man could go mad . . ., "Aaah."

Dylan lowered herself onto him again. She'd complete her ride of love this time. Adam held her there, impaled on the strength of him, barring her escape. She exclaimed her victory, as she straddled him, plunging them both into a vortex of pure sensation. Their bodies, wet from exertion glistened palely as they were painted by the sunlight that streamed through the balcony doors from a sun nearly set. They lay trembling from spent passion. Dylan felt a lethargy steal over her, invading her limbs and her mind as she nestled down next to Adam, wanting nothing more than to lie quietly next to him, while their seething emotions slowly returned to normal. Her mind registered she'd only have a short time before she had to leave for the airport. Her eyelids felt so heavy . . .

Dylan made her flight with only seconds to spare. She was still feeling highly emotional and having to rush around so as not to miss her flight put her in a teary frame of mind. She didn't want to leave and was having trouble holding her tears at bay, when they said their good-byes. She hugged him desperately, telling him through her tears, "I love you," before turning to walk quickly to her waiting flight.

She was mournfully contemplating more time spent without Adam by her side when she happened to overhear the two men across the aisle talking. Her curiosity was well and truly roused when she heard Adam's name mentioned, in conjunction with another woman.

"Are you sure it was him?" the second man wanted to know.

"Yes, he sure is a busy lad. A mate of mine saw him the other night with someone. He reckons they were joined at the hip. What I wouldn't give to be in his shoes. I bet he scored big that night." Typical male laughter followed these taunts, before they changed the subject.

Dylan felt her insides start to heave as she took in those hateful words. Hearsay, she told herself, probably just hearsay. They could be talking about the night the cast had eaten together at the restaurant. If so, that fiasco had been cleared up and forgotten, but still a nagging doubt festered within her heart. She looked at the gleaming ring on her finger and forcefully put the hateful words out of her mind. What did two strangers know about Adam? What did it all add up to? *Nothing,* Dylan told herself practically. It was very difficult to dispute rumours once they'd been started. Adam had already told her that on numerous occasions. The best thing to do he had said was to go on with life as if they didn't exist. He'd gone on to say that most rumours died a quiet death leaving him free to get on with his life. As for the others, well, he had a very good lawyer who took care of things like that for him.

Chapter Eight

"Look at the size of that rock!" Rae exclaimed, as she examined the diamond on Dylan's finger, "I hardly need to ask if the week-end was a success, do I?"

"No, you don't," Dylan answered gaily. She was in her usual morning rush, having brought the gang over to Rae's on her way to work.

"Are you going to hand in your notice now?" Rae knew of Dylan's reluctance to give up her work.

"I don't . . . ," Dylan began, but one look at Rae's set features had her changing her mind, "Alright, I'll do it."

"I'm sure if you feel so strongly about working, maybe you could get a job in America. Hey, I know, you could work with Adam, be his assistant and chase all of his over-sexed co-stars away with a big stick, that sort of thing." Rae wasn't one to let you wallow in your own misery. She believed you had to face your problems and deal with them. Even joking as she was now, her words held an element of truth to them.

"Behave," Dylan scolded her friend, as she bent down to quickly kiss her offspring, before scooting out the door, "I'll talk to you later, okay," she called over her shoulder to Rae. She was going to be late, if she didn't hurry.

"I'll be here. You can stay for tea. I want details!" yelled Rae, chuckling to herself, satisfied with the outcome of her friend's visit to the big smoke.

"What's her name again?" Rae wanted to know. They were sitting at the dinner table, empty plates everywhere. Tom and the children had gone outside, leaving the two women alone to talk.

"Sara Longston. She's beautiful. Straight out of a magazine, you know, lovely long hair, brown eyes and a figure I'd kill for. She'd look good in a potato sack," Dylan finished glumly.

"She might be good to look at by the sound of her, but if you ask me, that's all there is to her. I'd say she's been chasing Adam around without any luck and then you come along and really mucked things up for her. You're going to have to trust him if you love him," Rae pointed out, yet again.

"I know you're right, but I worry just the same. I can't help it. If I lost him, I don't know what I'd do."

"There's no chance of that ever happening, judging by the size of that rock on your finger," Rae indicated, picking up her friend's hand to look at her engagement ring yet again.

"It is beautiful, isn't it," Dylan agreed.

Conversation between them was brought to an abrupt halt as Dylan's children came running into the room, each of them clamouring for her attention.

"Uncle Tom took us riding, Mummy. Even Natalie had a go and do you know what? She didn't fall off once," Danny told his mother. Dylan could hear the pride in his young voice as he related this piece of news to her about his sister.

"I'm glad to hear it, Sweetheart," Dylan answered, trying to keep the smile from her face. Her gaze focused on Natalie, how she was growing up. No longer a baby, but still she . . .

"Mummy, I've been talking to you!" Dylan's thoughts were interrupted by a little hand shaking her arm. She looked down to see Glen at her side.

"I'm sorry, Sweetie, what were you saying?" she gently ruffled his hair and gave him her undivided attention.

"We helped milk the cows, but Natalie fell into one of the buckets and got milk all over her. Shep and her puppies came and drank it all up, before we could pick it up."

Natalie, who had been sitting on Dylan's lap, said in her own defence, "Pushed me," and pointed to Glen.

"I did not, you tripped," yelled Glen, quick to defend himself.

"Sounds like I missed all the fun," Dylan mused, looking over towards Rae.

"Yeah, but I bet you had a better time," Rae whispered into her ear, as she walked past her chair on her way to the sink.

Dylan had the grace to blush. Rae was hopeless, but Dylan couldn't have wished for a better friend. The bond of friendship that existed between them had them securely tied together for life.

The day Dylan had been patiently waiting for finally arrived. Adam had finished working and was now free to stay permanently with her, until they both left to start their new life in America. Dylan had also finished at the library, bidding her work mates a tearful good-bye. She'd been given excellent references; so hopefully, if the need arose she'd be able to find work.

"How long before you have to be back?" Dylan asked, as she arranged his underwear next to hers in the wardrobe. It gave his stay an added touch of permanency that she'd never felt before.

"About a month, maybe more, when do you pick up your passports?" he asked, poking his head around the wardrobe door.

"The end of the week," Glancing at her watch, Dylan told him, "I have to get Danny from school then pick up Natalie and Glen from Rae's. Come with me and then we can stay for a while."

They ended up staying for tea, discussing among other things, Dylan's eminent departure from the country.

"Sing out if you need anything done," Rae volunteered and then added, "Have you seen Jake? Won't he have to see the kids before you leave? It's only fair, Dylan."

"I know. I've been putting it off," Dylan stated glumly. If her ex-husband caused a stir, it would make leaving all that much harder emotionally, especially for their children.

"I'll come with you. We can go Tuesday. I won't be free until then. Go and ring him now to arrange it," Rae wasn't one to let the grass grow under her feet. Also, she knew if Dylan was given the time to think about it, she'd change her mind.

"What's wrong with me going with her?" Adam asked, while Dylan was out of the room, "I'm house trained."

"Barely," Rae smiled, before adding seriously, "I know it's frustrating for you, but I really think I should be the one to go with her. Jake won't like having you thrust in his face, believe me."

Adam gave in reluctantly, realising Rae was probably right. "But if he hurts her in any way . . . ," Adam left the rest of his words hanging in the air, unspoken, letting Rae and Tom draw their own conclusions as to his meaning.

Jake opened his door to them, smiling warmly when he saw his two younger children. He ushered the two women inside, indicating for them to sit down on the couch. He produced sweets for Glen and Natalie, bringing smiles to their young faces.

"I suppose you know why I'm here?" Dylan said quietly. She wanted to save Jake any pain. She felt guilty for taking his children to a part of the world where he wouldn't have access to them as readily as he would here. Not that he ever took advantage of this fact anyway.

"Yes, I guess I do," Jake told Dylan reluctantly.

Dylan continued nervously, "Jake, I want to take the children with me, naturally. I know it means you won't be able to see them very much, but please don't make it difficult for us." She had to swallow the lump in her throat that was threatening to choke her.

"Believe it or not, Dylan, I love my kids and only want what's best for them. I've given the matter a lot of thought and believe me, I thought of fighting you for them, but my conduct over the past few tears would go against me and you'd win in the end, so I'll do it your way. I won't fight you, Dylan," Dylan heard the emotion welling up in his voice and knew what it must have cost him to utter those words. He added huskily, "Just promise me that you'll keep in touch."

"Yes," was all she could get past the lump in her throat. They stayed a little while longer, giving him some time with Glen and

Natalie, until Dylan told him it was time to pick Danny up from school.

"Good-bye, Jake," Dylan said, giving him her hand. She sounded so stiff and formal even to her own ears.

"Good-bye, Dylan," he answered, ignoring her outstretched hand, instead drawing her to himself to kiss her on the cheek, "It wasn't a complete waste of time, was it?"

"No, not completely. We had some happy times," she answered huskily. Once they were in the car and driving away, she let the tears fall unchecked down her pale cheeks.

"Are there any regrets, Dylan?" Rae asked quietly, seeing the tears.

"No, I haven't got any regrets," Dylan assured her friend. "I wish Jake all the best. He just threw me, that's all. I was expecting a battle . . . you know."

"Yes, I know. I must say, I was impressed," Rae declared, thoughtfully, although not fully convinced as to Dylan's ex-husband's sincerity.

Over the next few days, Dylan started to go through her belongings. With Adam's help, she was able to weed out all of the rubbish from the things she wanted to keep. She hadn't realised just how much she'd accumulated over the years. There were bits and pieces from different stages of her life. Things she'd saved belonging to the boys and to Natalie. Adam teased her when he came across a yellowing envelope containing hair from Danny's first haircut.

"What's this?" he asked, holding the packet cautiously between his forefinger and thumb.

"That," said Dylan defensively, "is some of Danny's hair. I guess I'm overly sentimental. I suppose we can throw it away." She proceeded to do just that, putting it in with the growing pile of rubbish in the box beside them.

"Hey, you don't have to do that!" Adam admonished her, fishing the worn envelope back out of the box. Taking her hands tenderly between his own, he stated, "I don't expect you to get rid of anything. Hell, you can keep the whole damn lot if you want to, you know that!"

"Yes, I know. Anyway, it's time I went through all of this . . . ," she paused, trying to think of a suitable word that would describe all of the mess that was spread out around them and smiling wistfully, she added, "these memories."

They came across some snapshots of Jake and herself taken in happier times. "What about these?" Adam asked, using a tone of voice that caused Dylan to glance up from the pile of papers she'd been going through to see what he was referring to.

She took the snaps from Adam's hand to look at them. She was in Jake's arms, gazing up at him and it was apparent to anyone who cared to look, that they were in love.

"These were taken on our honeymoon," she answered Adam's unspoken question, continuing to gaze at the two people pictured there, wondering where they'd disappeared to. They'd had so many dreams, but their dreams had gone, never to return. Everything had died with the failure of their marriage. Tears filled her eyes and actually started to trickle down her cheeks.

"Tears, Dylan. Are you sorry it's over?" Adam asked quietly. His voice had a huskiness about it that tore at Dylan's heart.

"I was, once, long ago. No, my tears are for them." She nodded to the couple in the photo, "They could have had it all, but they ended up with nothing." She caught her breath, as she wiped the tears from her eyes. She smiled weakly at Adam, before telling him in a voice that wasn't quite steady, "What I felt for Jake . . . although I thought I loved him at the time; no, that's not right, I did love him at the time," she corrected herself before continuing, "It's not a fraction of the love I feel for you. With you, I feel so alive, so vibrant, it's different. I can't explain it." Dylan crawled across the short space to where Adam knelt; she needed to be near him, to touch him.

Realising Dylan's need to be comforted and if he was to analyse his own feelings, Adam knew he, also, needed to feel secure at the moment, he took Dylan in his arms, raining light kisses over her face and neck. Dylan brought her lips up to meet his, wanting nothing more than to be loved by this man. She slowly started to unbutton his shirt, wanting nothing to be between them. She wanted to feel the strength of him. She traced feather light patterns across his chest with the delicate tips of her fingers, gradually moving down the length of him, until she could feel the outline of his manhood as it strained against the zipper of his jeans. Adam's groans announced his evident need for her, while his own hands roamed over her fevered body, bringing her to throbbing vibrant life.

He kissed her face; his tongue licked her lips, igniting fires deep inside her, taking her on a much loved journey, one they'd travelled together before in complete harmony. His hot breath fanned her cheek as he made his way with exquisite thoroughness over her face, covering the distance to her ear, where he delved his tongue into the shell-like recess, before bringing his mouth back to once again take possession of her waiting lips. His kiss was full of all the longing he was feeling. His hands began a journey they knew well, they knew all of her hidden places that were there only for him. He visited them all, sending her into a delightful frenzy, moving first over her breasts, giving Dylan untold pleasure, before they continued their downward path over her stomach towards her mound of love. Slowly, lifting her blouse, Adam gently slipped his hand inside her jeans, levering them down over her slim hips until they were out of the way. He then moved his hand slowly inside her panties, until he reached her most secret place, the core of her love. Dylan was ready for him, already moist from his attention to her body. She emitted a husky groan of pure pleasure as Adam gently stroked the source of her sexual desire. Moving against him, as his hand continued its amorous adventure, Dylan's body throbbed as she gave in to the onslaught of passion that flooded her. Kissing his body wantonly, she cried out in rapturous joy as wave after wave of ecstasy swamped her, making her body sing with untold pleasure.

Wanting to give Adam the same pleasure he'd bestowed on her, Dylan started to plant light kisses on his chest. Blazing a trail downwards, towards the top of his jeans, she heard his intake of breath, as she slowly moved her fingers ever so lightly over him. She undid the top of his jeans, releasing his throbbing manhood from its jail to gaze lovingly upon him, before she slowly lowered her head to bestow kisses on the magnificence that was Adam.

"Dylan," Adam groaned, unable to hold back the flow of life as his body, caught in passionate tremors, released its essence.

Later, sharing coffee, they heard a car pull into the driveway, and then Dylan's three children came bounding up the stairs followed closely by Rae and Tom. The boys and Natalie had spent the day at the dairy leaving Dylan free to sort through her belongings.

"Mummy, Uncle Adam, Aunty Rae let me milk one of the cows again. I drank the milk, too, it was nice. Why can't we have a cow? We could keep it in the back yard," Danny pleaded, looking from one adult to the other, trying to gauge what their reaction would be to this small request.

"I'm sorry, Sweetheart, but we haven't got room for a cow, you know that. Anyway, we'll be leaving soon, had you forgotten?" Dylan answered, gazing fondly at her eldest son.

"Oh, yes, that's right. We're going to be rich, aren't we?" Danny replied with the innocence of a child.

"Danny!" Dylan admonished sternly, "Who told you that?"

Not knowing what he'd said that was wrong, Danny answered simply, "Richard. He said you'd landed on your feet. When did you fall down, Mummy?"

Dylan felt the anger rising within her, making it impossible for her to answer. She clutched Adam's hand tightly, trying unsuccessfully to bring herself under control.

"It means, son, that they're happy for your mom, okay," Adam answered, giving the child an explanation that he thought he'd understand. Satisfied with this explanation, Danny went off happily, going downstairs to play with his brother.

The four adults in the room looked at each other in silence, all of them keeping their own council as to what they were thinking. Dylan broke the silence, by saying with a sigh, "Well, it's started. I must say I'm not surprised by the source, either." She was hurt by this callous remark, obviously spoken so cattishly about her relationship with Adam. Richard was the son of her neighbour, Jo.

Adam cradled Dylan in his arms, telling her not to worry about people like Jo. He said they weren't worth the effort.

"I agree," Rae chimed in, determined to stop her friend's morale from dropping any lower, "Listen, how about we have a bar-b-que tonight. It can be for . . . um," Rae searched her mind, wanting a happy occasion. She had it, "It can be an engagement party and absolutely no sad sacks allowed, got it.' She looked at Dylan, daring her to disagree.

"Sounds great to me," Dylan replied cheerfully to the trio who stood watching her, "What are we waiting for?"

Dylan loved the peace they shared, as later in the week, she thought of the happiness Adam's being here had brought her. They hadn't been out, or done anything special, but just by his presence, he'd highlighted their time together. She looked out of the kitchen window to where the boys were building sand castles. Natalie toddled over to join them and was immediately shooed away, none too gently. The boys were about to pounce on her when they happened to glance up, seeing their mother looking at them from the window. Dylan slowly shook her head saying, "No."

"But, Mummy, she breaks everything," they wailed beseechingly, trying to win her over.

"Who breaks everything?" said a deep voice from behind her and two grubby hands came to rest easily on her shoulders.

"Natalie, poor little pet, the boys are playing in the sand pit. She keeps breaking in on them. She's got no one to play with," Dylan looked affectionately at her little girl. She was covered in sand, the pretty ribbon Dylan had put in her hair that morning was more off than on, her clean dress was dirty and had a tear in it, but to Dylan she looked beautiful.

"I've finished the car now, have I time before lunch to go down and play with them?" Before Dylan could answer, Adam went down on his knees and putting his hands over his face, cried melodramatically, "Please, Mommy, please. I'll be good, please."

"Yes, you idiot, please, do," Dylan giggled at his antics, as she pushed him out of the kitchen. Honestly, there were times when she wondered who the biggest kid was.

With that, Adam scrambled up, gave her a quick kiss and then went outside. When he reached the children, he scooped Natalie up into his arms, putting her onto his broad shoulders, making her laugh gleefully. Dylan's attention was diverted by someone walking up the front steps. She turned to see Rae walking towards her.

"Hi, I had some time to kill. Feel like a cuppa?" Rae asked her friend, as she walked towards the kitchen bench to turn the kettle on.

"What gives? I thought we were coming over to your place?" Dylan asked, as she watched Rae flit around the kitchen, getting the tea things ready.

"You are, but does that mean I can't come over now, as well? Pretty soon I won't see you at all, will I?"

'We'll keep in touch Rae, you know that. You can't get rid of me that easily. You're like family to me," Dylan told her friend and coming to stand in front of her, she enveloped her in a friendly hug, telling her that she'd be badly missed.

"Oh, shut up, you'll have me crying in a minute. Where's Adam?" she asked abruptly, changing the subject.

"He's outside playing with the kids. I don't know who's having the most fun, him or them," Dylan confessed, indicating the foursome outside.

"I'm glad for them. It's been a long time since they've had someone, a male, to care about them. Someone who doesn't care about getting dirty, or giving them his undivided attention."

"Yes, I know, but Rae as much as I love him, there are times when I get so scared. What if . . . ," Rae went to interrupt, "No, please, let me finish," Dylan overrode her friend's interference, "What if it fails? What if he just turned and walked away? It's not only me who'd be hurt. The children all love him, especially Natalie. Do you know she's started to call him daddy? She's never called Jake that. Look at them together out there."

"I knew about the daddy bit, she talks about her daddy all the time. I knew she didn't mean Jake. Dylan, I can only tell you to follow your heart. If you could only see the two of you together, I don't know, you look right. I'd bet everything I have that he loves you. You get on so well. I've never seen you look so happy and contented," Rae told her friend sincerely. She continued, "I can't understand your fear. Believe me, he loves you very much. As a matter of fact, he told me so just the other day, so I think you can lay your fears to rest."

"Adam told you he loves me . . . when?" Dylan was astounded by this announcement from her friend.

"When you were over the other day, remember you and Tom went to look at the new colt? Well, my friend, Adam and I had quite a heart to heart," Rae answered smugly, looking at Dylan from over the rim of her teacup.

"But what did he say?" Dylan demanded, knowing she didn't have an iceberg's chance in hell of coercing Rae into telling her if she didn't want to. She'd just have to accept what her friend had told her as being the truth.

"I told you, he loves you. Have no fears about that. He said he's never been happier, okay"

"Okay," repeated Dylan happily.

Their talk was interrupted by what sounded like an army storming up the back steps. They both turned to see Adam, Danny, Glen and Natalie racing into the laundry, covered in sand from head to foot.

"Hold it, you lot! Where do you think you're going?" Dylan stated sternly, trying to keep the merriment out of her voice.

Four pairs of eyes looked at her from behind sand covered faces, before Glen said, "Into the bedroom, to play with our cars. Daddy Adam said he'd help us set up the race track."

"Oh, he did, did he? Well, not like that, you're not. I hate to bring this small fact to your attention, but you're all covered in sand. Just what have you been doing?" Dylan was hard put to keep the severity in her voice. Natalie was hiding behind Adam and was actually peering out at her from between his long legs.

"Nothing, we took it in turns to bury each other in the sand, that's all," ventured Danny innocently, as if it was a common occurrence to be buried in sand.

"Out!" said Dylan, pointing to the door, "Get those clothes off before you come in here. I've just cleaned."

"I told you she'd crack up, didn't I," Adam said to his partners in crime, as they trudged back outside. He pushed the children outside, then poked his head around the door to tell Dylan seriously, "I love a woman whose masterful," then winked at her outrageously before going back downstairs himself.

Dylan turned to Rae who had a ridiculous smirk plastered over her face. She said as they both burst out laughing, "See what I mean?"

"Surely that puts your mind at rest anyway?" Rae murmured, when she was able to speak properly.

"Yes, I guess so," Dylan agreed.

Getting up from her chair, Rae sighed, "Well, I guess I'd better be getting back. Tom will be wondering where I am. He was out in the paddock when I left."

"You mad thing, do you mean to tell me you dropped everything and came over here on the spur of the moment?" Dylan asked, glancing at Rae as if she'd gone mad.

"Yep, 'fraid so," Rae declared, walking from the room. Her eyes were suspiciously bright as she fought back the tears that were threatening to fall.

Later that day Adam was helping Dylan to do some more packing. They were sitting on the lounge room floor surrounded by packing boxes. Some of Dylan's paintings had been taken down from the wall ready to be wrapped and packed away ready to be shipped to Adam's home in America. Dylan found herself wondering yet again why she was taking all of this stuff with her when it would have been a lot easier to just refurnish, buying everything she needed when she arrived in America.

"Adam, I really don't need to take all of this stuff with me. Why won't you let me leave it here with Rae and Tom? They don't mind and have said they'll keep it for me." Dylan asked him yet again. They'd had this particular conversation many times before.

"Because it belongs to you and I want you to have it with you. End of story, okay," Adam was adamant and wouldn't budge from the decision he'd made. "And if I don't see every bit of this stuff when we get home you'll be in trouble, get it?"

Dylan sighed, giving in gracefully. "Okay, if you insist," It was useless to try to talk him out of this particular decision. His mind was well and truly made up and to be honest she did want to take it all with her.

"Is this a new painting?" he asked changing the subject while looking intently at the painting before him. "I don't remember seeing it before."

Dylan took her lead from him and veered away from the subject of her belongings and concentrated on the painting he now held in his hands. "Yes, it's new. It's good, isn't it?" Dylan told him. She'd purchased this particular painting at an art gallery exhibition a few weeks ago. It was to have been hung next to her mother's paintings, but due to her imminent departure from the country she hadn't seen the sense of putting it on the wall only to take it down after so short a time. The exhibition had been held at the library where she worked, or more precisely in the art gallery that was attached to the library, but they were all happy families working together. She was surprised that Adam noticed it at all. She hadn't thought he'd taken particular notice of her art collection.

"Is it one of your mother's?"

"No. It's by an artist called Marie Seeman. It's actually a drawing because she's used pastels as her medium of choice. That's why when it was framed she's put a glass covering over it as well. It protects the painting."

Adam merely nodded waiting for her to continue. He found he was interested.

"She's a new artist and if I'm any judge she has a bright future ahead of her. One day the world will recognise the name Marie Seeman and bow down to it. I'm glad I was able to get one of her paintings now while they're still selling at a reasonable price. Her popularity will send the price of her artwork through the roof. You mark my words." Dylan wished Marie well because working in the library as she did, or rather as she had, she corrected herself, she had gone to various art exhibitions and book launches so she knew first-hand how hard it could be for artist's to get established in their chosen field.

Dylan looked at the painting through fresh eyes. Marie had chosen her palette wisely using her pastels to their best advantage. Strong yellows, oranges, browns and greens had been used to depict grasses, bushes and various tufts of vegetation that grew along the side of the road. Dark storm clouds were starting to gather obliterating the blue sky making the onlooker aware that rain was possibly not all that far away. All in all Dylan thought it was a striking representation of a country road seen in its natural state through the eyes of the artist. It suited Dylan's taste completely and she had bought it knowing it would hang comfortably amongst her other art treasures.

Dylan was staring at the drawing absorbing the atmosphere it was showing her. Her imagination carried her to this lonely place in the middle of god only knew where. The little country road meandered off into the distance and was partly obscured here and there by the tall spiky grass that had been left to grow wild as nature had intended. She could clearly make out the tiny seeds growing on the tips of the long blades of grass and imagined them being gently blown away by a soft summer breeze thereby giving the promise of new growth. She thought it would be nice to walk along that white sandy track which would take her to who knows where . . . possibly to Adam? Yes, she decided smiling softly; it would definitely take her to Adam. He was sitting waiting for her just around the bend in that gently curving country road. He had a picnic ready and waiting for her, but she had better hurry because those storm clouds looked like they weren't about to wait too much longer for her.

Dylan sighed liking the daydream she had created for herself and was almost sorry to be back in the real world. The only thing that made it bearable was that Adam was here with her in the land of the living. She wondered if Adam would like to go on a picnic. She looked across at him and was disconcerted to find him looking at her with a wry grin plastered on his face almost as if he had been able to read her thoughts. *Well, they had been good thoughts,* she conceded to herself.

"What?" she asked him hoping that she hadn't been wearing any goofy expressions as she thought of their time together behind the bend in that country road.

"Nothing," he told her simply while smiling his sexy smile at her.

Dylan felt she had to explain. "I was just thinking about what was around the corner of that country road. We were having a picnic," she told him hoping he wouldn't laugh at her. Her eyes had misted over with a fine sheen of tears. "I know I'm stupid and you can laugh if you want to." But she hoped that he wouldn't.

"I like picnic's," was all he said as he reached for her, pulling her into his arms to hold her securely, thinking that he never wanted to let her go.

No sooner were they home from Rae and Tom's, following a delicious bar-be-que, than the phone started to ring. Answering it, Dylan found it was for Adam. He was putting Natalie to bed; a ritual the little girl loved him to do every night.

"Adam, you're wanted on the phone," Dylan called to him, wondering who it could be.

They passed in the hallway, Adam on his way to take his call, while Dylan went to finish putting Natalie to bed. Adam gave her a quick kiss as they passed each other.

Dylan didn't hear what was being said, not that she worried about it; she knew Adam would tell her if she wanted to know what the conversation had been about.

Adam was in the kitchen making them a cup of coffee. "Did she go down alright?"

"After a while, I had to finish a story you'd been telling her. Just what does the Million Man do anyway?"

Adam chuckled, "The Million Man. It's the Chameleon Man. He can be anything you want him to be. My dad used to tell me stories when I was a kid. He used to say he could change shape, colour and form, anything, just like the real thing."

"Judging from today's episode in the sand pit, I'd say that wasn't all that long ago," Dylan joked, coming over to put her arms around him. She could smell the faint tang of his after shave on his clothes; it reminded her of musk sticks.

"Yeah, you could be right," Adam agreed, resting his head lightly on top of hers, while he ran his hands along the length of her backbone absently. He took a deep breath before continuing, "I have something to tell you about that phone call."

"What?" Dylan could feel her body starting to tighten, as she stood waiting. She tried to move away from Adam's light clasp, but he tightened his hold on her.

"I have to fly down to Melbourne. There's a producer there who wants to talk to me. Apparently, he can't come up here, because he has other people to see. He's on a tight schedule," Adam told her, knowing the reaction this piece of news would create.

Dylan felt as if someone had turned out the lights to her heart. She heard herself ask, "When? When do you have to go?" She could feel the tears starting to form in her eyes.

"Honey, don't. It won't be for long. Probably just overnight," Adam stated consolingly, pulling her tighter in to his firm body.

"I know. I'm being stupid," murmured Dylan into his chest. She tried to push herself away, but this action only made Adam hold her tighter as he tried to explain.

"Dylan, meetings like this are a part of my job. Admittedly, I wouldn't normally do something like this at home, fly out to meet them, but if this meeting pays off, it could mean doing another movie out here if I like the deal they're offering."

"It's alright, really," she sought to put his mind at rest; "I'm being selfish. I wanted you to myself a bit longer, that's all. I haven't wanted anything to spoil our time together. It will probably never be this quiet again. I've kind of looked on this time we've spent together as a sort of honeymoon."

"A honeymoon!" Adam said, surprised by this admission. He then added thoughtfully, "It has been great, but I kinda' thought of our honeymoon a bit differently though. You know, Desert Island, no children, no people, no clothes . . . that sort of thing."

Dylan was forced to laugh against her will. The latter part of Adam's speech was delivered with such innocence and with a completely bland expression; Dylan knew he was trying to cheer her up. She had no choice, but to play along with him. She looked up at him coyly as she said, "You'll have to teach me the etiquette of living on a desert island. It might take me a few good lessons until I get it right. Are you up to the challenge, Mister Rossiter?"

"Always, my Love, always," he whispered into her ear as he led her towards the bedroom.

Even for a Saturday morning, the traffic didn't seem to be very heavy. Dylan drove into the hotel car park, easily finding a space. Her small car looked out of place among the more elite vehicles parked there.

Adam had arrived back late last night, but had chosen to stay at the airport hotel rather than make the long journey out to the bay. He'd explained over the phone that he'd had an early morning meeting and therefore couldn't see the sense of coming home, only to turn around and come back into the city, within the space of a few hours.

Easily finding the room number, Dylan was about to knock when she changed her mind, deciding to surprise Adam by just walking in on him. The door was unlocked, he was expecting her and so she quietly let herself in. She could hear voices, one of them belonged to a woman, the only other voice in the room belonged to Adam. Both voices were raised in anger. The woman had just asked him if he was going to tell his wife about them, so they could be married. She sounded anguished, in pain.

Adam cut her off, shouting violently. Dylan therefore hadn't the slightest bit of difficulty in hearing his harsh, cruel words. "I told you in the beginning I'd never leave her. It suits me to stay with her, the fact that I don't love her makes not the slightest bit of difference, nor does the fact that you're pregnant. Aren't there clinics for that sort of thing these days? Did you think you'd be able to trap me by having a kid?" Dylan heard a slap and she presumed someone was being hit and then the woman was sobbing, pleading with him to stop, to help her.

Dylan was trembling uncontrollably by this time, she'd heard enough. She knew if she had any sense she should go and get help, but escape was uppermost in her mind, she had to get away. She left the room as quietly as she'd entered it, feeling like a wounded animal, wanting only to be left alone to lick her wounds.

Her actions were automatic as she made her way back to her car. Once there, she was unable to move, her mind kept going back over the conversation she'd just heard. *All this time,* she thought, *all this time it's only been a sham to him, a game he'd been playing with her emotions.* He could have someone like her everywhere he went, although she doubted anyone else was as gullible as she appeared to be.

Well, she thought miserably as she manoeuvred her car out into the traffic, *at least I found out in time before I married him, but the other woman thinks we're already married. He probably told her he was married to save himself any problems now or with anyone he fancied having an affair with in the future. By marrying me, he's got himself a safety net just in case anyone tries to get too close. And the children, they were the perfect foil against any attempt to get a divorce. All he had to do was say he couldn't bear to be parted from his children. Dylan thought she had it all figured out. He needed her, to use her and her family as a buffer to fall back on. How could he do this to her, when she loved him so completely.*

Finally the tears that had been threatening to fall cascaded down her cheeks. They scalded her eyes, making driving difficult, but still she continued, wanting to put as much distance between her and that horrible scene as she could. I should have confronted him there in the hotel room while he was still with his lover, then it would be all behind me now, I wouldn't have to face him. *I won't face him,* she shuddered thinking that was an ordeal she wouldn't put herself through. She'd leave, coming home only when she knew he'd gone . . .

Dylan's thoughts were interrupted by the blaring of a car horn somewhere close at hand. She didn't take any notice and realised too late, she'd driven through a red light and was now in the path of an oncoming truck that had nowhere else to go, except to plough straight into her. She heard a sickening crunch as her car was hit, sending it careering sideways along the road, while at the same time, she felt agonising pain spreading throughout her whole body, bringing with it unconsciousness and mercifully for the moment, Dylan knew no more as her mind was cloaked with relieving blackness.

It was some time later when Rae's phone rang. She was puzzled to hear Adam's voice coming over the line. He sounded concerned.

"Rae, Adam here. Dylan wouldn't be there by any chance, would she?"

"Adam, I thought . . . I mean, where are you?" Rae's voice showed her confusion.

"Still at the hotel; is anything wrong? Dylan was supposed to meet me here hours ago," Adam stated. He ran his long fingers through his hair, distracted by the thought of Dylan not picking him up. "I tried her cell phone, but as usual it went to message bank."

Rae felt a cold chill course through her as she apprehensively told him, "She left here hours ago to pick you up. I've been to the beach with the kids, when you weren't here when we got back, I assumed you'd gone to Dylan's place for a while."

"She hasn't turned up here. Where in hell is she?" Rae could hear the concern in Adam's voice.

"I don't know what's happened, Adam, but I'm sure everything's fine," Rae assured him, while her own stomach was churning with an unknown fear, "She's probably broken down and cursing that car of hers. Can you get out here?"

"I'll be there as soon as I can," he replaced the receiver, before she could say anything more. Dylan had been having trouble with the car, but he'd fixed most of the problems and the others shouldn't have caused any major breakdowns. At least, he didn't think so.

Rae had no sooner related the story to Tom when the phone rang again. Tom rose to answer it, saying with a grin, "I bet that's Dylan now. She'll be as angry as hell if it is the car."

Dylan's head throbbed as she opened her eyes, at first she couldn't remember what had happened to her, but as realisation came flooding back so, too, did memories of Adam. She'd been thinking of him, instead of concentrating on her driving. She'd seen the truck too late and was unable to manoeuvre her car out of its oncoming path, both vehicles had hit, hers being the smaller of the two, had borne the brunt of the damage. And it seemed the same could be said of herself.

Dylan looked down at herself, slowly moving her arms and legs, trying to establish if any bones were broken. She ached all over, but thankfully there didn't seem to be any bandages or plaster casts covering her. She gingerly lifted a shaky hand to her head, wincing instantly as her fingers came into contact with a bandage that was wrapped around her skull. She feebly attempted to attract the attention of a passing nurse, "Please, can you help me?"

"Certainly, it's good to see you awake, that's a good sign," the nurse told her, as she stood by Dylan's bed.

"How did I get here? I don't remember anything after being hit. I blacked out," Dylan wondered how long she'd been here, it could have been days. Had they been able to contact her family, did everyone know about the accident?

"You have concussion, plus some minor cuts and bruises. Also, a very nasty cut on your head that required several stitches. You're very lucky to be alive, according to the police. They don't know how you weren't killed," the nurse patted Dylan's hand sympathetically, "You must have somebody up there looking after your wellbeing." She thought it was good to get an accident victim who actually survived for a change. She'd been told the young woman's car was a total wreck.

"Does anyone know? I mean . . . do you know who I am? My children . . . ," Dylan started to panic, although for what reason she couldn't have said.

"We had to go through the contents of your bag to find out your name. Your family have been contacted, Mrs Miles. Your friend is waiting outside, but she'll have to wait just a little while longer to see you, the doctor wanted to be notified as soon as you regained consciousness. I'll go and get him, but for now try to rest," her angel of mercy told her.

So Adam wasn't here. But then, did she really expect him to be? Dylan remembered thinking before she drifted back to sleep that it would be good to see Rae, to unburden herself of the load she was carrying. At least while she slept, she was granted a semblance of peace from her torrid thoughts about Adam.

When next she woke, it was to find Rae sitting by her bed. She was holding her hand gently within her own. "Rae!" she choked out, before bursting into tears. Rae let her cry, thinking the tears were about the accident. Dylan couldn't stop the flow once they'd started. She was trying to tell Rae about Adam, but her friend misunderstood, thinking Dylan wanted to see him, that she was asking for him.

"No! No!" she choked out so vehemently, Rae just looked at her, dumbfounded. She took several deep breaths to steady herself, before adding, "I don't want to see him, Rae, do you understand? Keep him away from me!" Dylan's feeble grasp had found a new strength, as she clasped Rae's hands, begging her friend to carry out her wishes.

Rae could see Dylan was on the point of hysteria and indeed several heads had turned in their direction to see if there was a problem.

"Calm down. Just tell me why you don't want to see him?" Rae was worried, could her friend have become totally deranged by the accident. There was certainly something she didn't know.

Dylan haltingly told Rae her story, finishing with, "I still love him, Rae, but I can't face him, not now. How could he use us,

Rae?" Dylan's voice broke and she lay quietly sobbing, her face pale and tear stained.

"You're right about one thing, it doesn't make any sense. Could you be mistaken?" Rae wanted to know, thoroughly confused by what she'd been told. She was determined to get to the bottom of this puzzle. She'd have to get to Adam before he saw Dylan. Adam and Tom were already on their way to the hospital. If Adam saw Dylan before Rae had clued him in, there could be worse trouble. It would be better if he was prepared, but if it turned out that Dylan was right! Rae pursed her lips at the thought. She'd left Tom at home to break the news to Adam and to bring him to the hospital. Rae's visit was cut short by the arrival of a doctor wishing to see Dylan. Rae was glad of the excuse; she'd wait outside for Adam to arrive.

Dylan's nerves had seen better times; she'd dozed off again after seeing the doctor. Apparently, the shock of the accident, plus her concussion were the main contributors for her sleepiness. It must have been visiting hours, because she noticed a steady file of visitors streaming past her doorway. As much as she didn't want to see Adam, a part of her craved his presence, willing him to appear. She was in the middle of a love-hate situation and she wasn't coping very well. She loved him so much, she was almost willing to overlook his extramarital exercises, but as soon as this thought entered her mind, she knew she could never share him, or his love, with another woman.

Dylan closed her eyes, trying to rid herself of these perjurious thoughts, but even with her eyes tightly shut, her mind conjured up his image, throwing his laughing face up at her, to torment her. Opening her eyes, Dylan was momentarily confused to see Adam standing in the doorway, watching her. Was he a figment of her imagination, brought to life to haunt her? No, he was real enough. He looked terrible, he was pale beneath his tan and Dylan could see small worry lines feathering out from his eyes and there was a whiteness around his mouth that Dylan hadn't seen before. He seemed uncertain of himself, as he stood there.

"Can I come in?" he wanted to know. She looked so fragile, but the doctors had reassured him she'd be back on her feet within a few days.

Dylan nodded, almost against her will. What was she doing letting him near her, didn't she have any pride at all where this man was concerned? Pain shot through her head, making her wince. She knew she should send him away, but lacked the courage to do so. She didn't know how she was going to get through this; her heart had started pounding at an alarming rate, making it hard for her to breathe. Did he know she knew of his treachery, or was he ignorant of the fact? She didn't know what she should say to him, so she remained silent, willing him to make the first move.

"Can I stay, Dylan?" his voice sounded strange, he spoke with a slight tremor, almost as if he was having difficulty getting the words out.

Dylan nodded her head again, not able to trust her voice. She had to hold her hands tightly clasped, in case she reached out to him, which was what she most wanted to do. She was in grave danger of bursting into tears.

"Please tell me what happened?" his deep masculine voice was low, full of raw emotion. "Help me to understand. Rae told me you went to the hotel." Adam grabbed her hands, holding them firmly clasped in his own capable, strong grip.

Bleak eyes looked up at him. She murmured, "If Rae has already clued you in, you . . . ," she choked on the words, unable to finish.

"Go on," Adam pushed her relentlessly, hurt yet again by her apparent lack of trust in him and his love for her. He let her go, smacking the fist of his right hand into the palm of his left hand. His green eyes flashed fire as he watched her. Rae had already bailed him up, giving him a bad time, telling him of Dylan's accusations. Damn him if this woman of his wouldn't drive him crazy one day. He resolved not to give in, they had to have it out and as much as he hated to do it, that time was going to be now.

Dylan jumped visibly, frightened momentarily by the change in him. She chokingly told her story a second time. She couldn't read the expression on his face; it was like trying to read a closed book.

Adam was silent long after Dylan had finished speaking. His green eyes glittered dangerously, like shards of ice, while he stood listening to Dylan's story. He was ominously quiet, not moving a muscle, except for a small pulse which was beating frantically at the side of his throat. She'd never seen him so angry, because that's what it was . . . pure, white, hot anger. She wondered if he was going to answer her at all. When she thought she couldn't stand the suspense any longer, he said calmly between stiff lips, "What you heard, Dylan, was an audition a friend of mine wanted me to do with his grand-daughter. I owed him a favour. I've told you before, love scenes are mechanical, you just do them. If you'd made yourself known, you would have seen a room full of people, behind the scenes, so to speak. I refused to go to the studio because I was waiting for you. I also wanted you to meet these people; they're friends of mine. If you can't trust me, Dylan, I don't see much of a future for us. This sort of thing is my job, it means nothing else," Adam's voice trailed off into nothingness, half in anger, half in desperation. He added, as an afterthought, "I don't know what else to add, so I'll leave now. Good-bye." He started to walk purposely from the room.

"Will you be back?" Dylan called after him, her voice catching in her throat. She was without pride where this man was concerned.

Adam stopped momentarily, half turning, but not quite facing Dylan as he answered, "I don't know," before he continued walking from the room. He held himself rigidly until he rounded the corner, then his broad shoulders slumped, as he leaned heavily against the wall. He ran shaking fingers through his hair, trying to understand how Dylan could think him capable of such a disparagement against their relationship.

After Adam's departure, Dylan couldn't stop her tears from falling. Because of her stupidity and petty jealousy, she'd lost the only man she'd ever truly love. She'd never felt so desolate, or alone in her entire life. She had to get him back. She didn't know how, but she was prepared to fight for him, if the need arose. Life without him would be meaningless. This was the first positive thought she'd had since the accident and she held on to it, afraid that if she let it go, she'd lose her resolve.

"He's mine and I want him back. I can't let him go, I love him," she determined to the empty room. Her head throbbed, as she tried unsuccessfully to get out of bed. A violent wave of nausea swept over her, almost threatening unconsciousness if she didn't slow down. She tried again moments later, she had to find him, to tell him, but it seemed that her own traitorous body, still very much weakened by the accident wouldn't take her where she wanted to go. "Adam," she muttered weakly, as she realised hopelessly that she couldn't follow him.

"I'm here, Sweetheart," came a voice from the doorway.

Dylan turned her head to see Adam leaning in the doorway, his tall frame nearly filling the space. Dylan looked up into his face, trying to gauge his feelings. Her own face, she knew, had turned a brilliant crimson from being overheard, but suddenly she didn't care. He was here, he hadn't left. She felt suddenly shy of this man she loved. She wanted so desperately to tell him she loved him, but the words wouldn't come, they stuck in her throat.

Instead, she found herself muttering, "Adam, I've been such a fool. Can you ever forgive me for ever doubting you?" Fresh tears started spilling down her cheeks.

In answer to her question, Adam strode across the room to take her into his strong arms. He held her protectively while she wept.

"What made you come . . . come back?" she asked, from the safety of his strong embrace. Her voice hiccupped, as she tried to bring it under control.

"I never left. I was sitting outside, trying to think of a way to come back in. It broke my heart to hear you crying, but you had to come to the conclusion that you wanted me by yourself. I'm glad you think I'm worth fighting for," his own eyes were suspiciously bright, as he related this last piece of information to her, "It gave me the opening I needed," he added gruffly.

"Oh, Adam," Dylan uttered. She held him, uncaring of the pain that shot through her limbs. Nothing was more important to her than Adam at that moment.

"Try to rest, Sweetheart," he told her, gently stroking her hands as he held them, mindful of not hurting her bruised body.

"Kiss me, please," Dylan asked softly, looking up at him. She needed to feel his lips on hers.

"I might hurt you," he told her uncertainly. She looked so frail, but he did so want to kiss her, to wash away all the unpleasantness of the last few hours.

"Please," Dylan pleaded, "I need you."

There was silence in the room for the next few minutes as Adam did as he was bidden, although he was mindful of Dylan's bruised body. Dylan kissed him hungrily, thinking as she did so how easily she could have lost him due to her stupidity. Never to have the pleasure of feeling his strong body next to hers again was something she never wanted to endure. She shuddered at the thought.

Adam broke their embrace and began to pace the floor, "Dylan, I have to talk about it, I'm sorry. I've never been so scared. When you didn't turn up, I thought perhaps you'd broken down, but when I arrived at the dairy and Tom told me about the accident . . . I don't ever want to feel that helpless, or that scared again. When we arrived here, Rae said you didn't want to see me, and then she tore strips off me for having a mistress . . . ," at this point, Adam's voice broke and he couldn't go on. He shrugged his shoulders turning away from her, standing with his hands in his pockets. His broad shoulders heaved as he took in a great lung full of air while he tried to deal with his own feelings. What he'd gone through during the long hours since this morning, she'd probably never know, she was aware of that.

Dylan felt his pain as her own. She was the cause of it, because of her lack of trust, she'd hurt this man. She struggled, as she tried to get out of bed, wincing as a jolt of pain shot through her head, causing her to gingerly place her head back onto the pillow.

Adam turned at her uttered cry of pain and then swiftly crossed to her bedside. "What do you think you're trying to do?" he asked her, as he settled her back under the covers.

"Trying to get to you," she confessed, as she let Adam fuss with the sheets, "I love you so very much, Adam. I'm sorry for not trusting you."

His answer was to kiss her longingly. Dylan lost herself in the magic of his kisses. His medicine was the best kind of all. She could gladly overdose on his nearness. Forgetting about her head, she returned his kisses ardently, losing herself completely. Much later, he told her he was going to marry her while she was still weak and groggy from the accident so she'd say yes before she'd realised what she'd done.

"I won't need to be weak, or groggy. You've got me for better or worse already." Dylan smiled up at him as she added affectionately, "You really are normal, aren't you?" It suddenly didn't matter where they lived, or if his lifestyle was grander than she was used to, or if his homes were bigger or better than hers. He'd proven to her countless times since she'd known him that he was completely down to earth in every way. He enjoyed the same simple pleasures as she did.

She was rewarded by an answering smile as she was told, "I like to think so."

She felt the nerves tighten in her stomach, as she thought of the extra piece of news that she had for him. This would be a test of his love for her surely. "There's something else I have to tell you. I guess now is as good a time as any, seeing I have your undivided attention," Dylan stopped suddenly, not knowing how to go about telling him. She wrung her hands together; this was going to be harder than she thought.

"Go on, Honey," he prompted, taking both of her hands in his, only to have her pull them out of his grasp again.

Dylan found she couldn't look at him. She fidgeted with the covers on the bed, absently pulling at the sheet. "Oh, hell, this is ridiculous," she said, more to herself than to him. Then, taking a deep breath, she blurted out, "It seems I'm pregnant! The doctors found out when they were checking me for injuries."

There was complete silence in the room. Dylan was forced to look up at Adam. He was looking at her like someone in shock. She knew it, he didn't want a baby.

"I'm sorry. I guess I should have been more careful. I didn't know, isn't that stupid!" she said, looking away again. She wanted this baby so much; it had been created because of their love for each other. She hadn't planned it; its conception had been an innocent accident. She was on the pill, using it to help regulate her period. Without it, she could never be sure when they'd arrive and they'd always be extremely heavy. The pill had helped to cure her of that particular problem, while at the same time, since meeting Adam, it had acted as a contraceptive; because of the pill she'd thought herself to be free of the possibility of ever falling pregnant with Adam's child. Since being informed of her pregnancy earlier today, she'd carefully gone over the events of the last few months in her mind, trying to figure out when they could have possibly conceived a child.

"A baby! Honey, are you sure?" Dylan's gaze was drawn back to Adam's face. He had a grin that stretched from ear to ear, "But how! I mean you take the pill, don't you?"

"Yes. I've been racking my brains trying to come up with a feasible explanation and I think I've found it." She looked up into his face, trying to gauge his reaction to her outburst.

"And," he prompted, keen to be let into the secret.

"The night Rae and the girls came over for a few drinks. Remember." at his nod, she continued, "I was sick because I'd had too much to drink. I probably threw the pill up with everything else. That would have left me unprotected for the rest of the month."

"But you had a period after that," he clearly remembered having to drive down to the local pharmacy, because she'd run out of tampons.

"Yes, but my period was very light. I thought it was because of stress. Obviously, I was mistaken."

"Oh, I didn't know something like that could happen," he told her matter-of-factly.

"Sometimes," she told him, before cautiously asking in a more sedate manner, "You're not ang . . . ," Adam quickly put his fingers gently over her mouth to stop her from uttering whatever it was she'd been going to say.

"No, I'm not. Sweetheart, that's great news," He placed his hands gently on her stomach. His child was, this very minute, growing there. His face clouded, as he had an awful thought, "The baby, is he safe? Have they told you?"

Dylan raised her eyebrows at him. "He . . . he, or she, is in perfect condition. The doctor checked me out. We're both fine."

"We'll get married as soon as possible. Now you'll have to marry me," he stated smugly, smiling down at her.

"Yes, I guess I will," Dylan agreed happily. She knew happiness beyond belief as they talked about their future together. She knew now she'd no longer be jealous of Adam's female co-stars or of his work. His heart would always be with her and their family. She was a woman in love who was loved in return by her man. She knew this would always be enough for her.

P.S. Madison Clare Rossiter was born on the 27th July 2012 at the Los Angeles County Hospital. She was 53 cms in length and weighed a healthy 7lb 14ounces.

Dylan and Adam are still happily married ☺

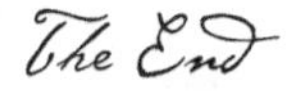

About The Author

About the author, hey. Okay, here we go then.

To date I have written 4 novels, three of which have now been published through Trafford - an American based self-publishing company to whom I will always be eternally grateful. This novel, **When Love Knocks**, is the fourth to be published, but it was the very first one to be written.

I'm a down to earth person with a simple philosophy which is, "Don't take yourself too seriously." I was born in Brisbane, the capital of Queensland here in Australia. I work full time as a disability support worker for a company here in Rockhampton. I moved to Rocky in 1989. I have been writing my stories since 1988. I'm divorced. I have 5 children and 11 grandchildren. I love being a grandmother.

I also volunteer my time at the local community radio station as an on-air announcer for 4 hours on a Saturday. I love playing music and hearing from members of the public who seem to phone me on a regular basis.

In 1992 or thereabouts I decided to further my education and entered Central Queensland University as a mature age student thinking that getting out into the world would give me an added bonus when it came to my writing. I have a Bachelor of Arts degree with majors in Literature, Drama, Journalism and Creative

Writing. From there, I went on to do a Graduate Diploma in Secondary teaching to become a high school teacher for a number of years until I decided to give it away to become a disability support worker. This is a job that I love.

My writing has always given me a sense of satisfaction. I love nothing better than giving my characters a happy ending. I have been reading romance novels since I was 16 and immediately fell under their spell.